"We're friends, aren't we, Blackie?"

Jeff knelt down and without hesitation the dog came to him, eagerly licking his face.

The man's eyes revealed fleeting surprise. "Blackie," he snapped. "Heel."

The Labrador squeezed between two overgrown laurel bushes and returned to his master, who didn't look any too pleased at his dog's affection for Jeff.

"My son has a way with animals," Robin explained. "By the way, I'm Robin Masterson, and this is my son, Jeff. We moved in yesterday."

"I'm Cole Camden. Welcome to the neighborhood." Although his words were cordial, his tone wasn't. And neither was the look on his face.

"I don't suppose you have any kids?" Jeff broke in excitedly.

Robin could have sworn the question angered Cole. An uncomfortable moment passed before he answered, his voice hard. "No, I don't have any kids." But for a split second, Robin was sure she saw a flash of pain in his eyes.

Debbie Macomber is an American writer living in the state of Washington. She has four children, all of them teenagers, and also supports a menagerie that includes cats, a dog and some guinea pigs. Debbie's successful writing career actually started in childhood, when her brother copied—and sold!—her diary. She's gone on to a considerably wider readership since, as a prolific and popular author published in several different romance lines. She says she wrote her first book because she fell in love with Harlequin Romance novels—and wanted to write her own.

Books by Debbie Macomber

HARLEQUIN ROMANCE

FATHER'S DAY
Debbie Macomber

Harlequin Books

TORONTO • NEW YORK • LONDON
AMSTERDAM • PARIS • SYDNEY • HAMBURG
STOCKHOLM • ATHENS • TOKYO • MILAN

ISBN 0-373-03130-0

Harlequin Romance first edition June 1991

For Lois and Bill Hoskins,
living proof that love is
better the second time around

FATHER'S DAY

CHAPTER ONE

"I CAN'T BELIEVE I'm doing this," Robin Masterson muttered as she crawled into the makeshift tent pitched over the clothesline in the backyard of her new home.

"Come on, Mom," ten-year-old Jeff urged, shifting to make room for her. "It's warm as toast in here."

Down on all fours, a flashlight in one hand, Robin squeezed her way inside. Jeff had constructed the flimsy tent using clothespins to hold up the blankets and rocks to secure the base. The space was tight, but she managed to maneuver her slim body into the sleeping bag.

"Isn't this great?" Jeff asked. He stuck his head out the front opening and gazed at the dark sky and the spattering of stars that winked back at them. On second thought Robin decided they were laughing at her, those stars. And with good reason. There probably wasn't another thirty-year-old woman in the entire state of California who would agree to this craziness.

It was the first night in their new house and Robin was exhausted to the bone. They'd started moving out of the apartment before five that morning and she'd just finished unpacking the last box. The beds were assembled, but Jeff wouldn't hear of doing anything as mundane as sleeping on a real mattress. After waiting years to camp out in his own backyard, her son wasn't about to delay the adventure by even one night.

Robin couldn't let him sleep outside alone, and since he hadn't met any neighbors yet, there was only one option left. Surely there would be a Mother of the Year award in this for her.

"You want to hear a joke?" Jeff asked, rolling onto his back and nudging her.

"Sure." She swallowed a yawn, hoping she could stay awake long enough to laugh at the appropriate time. She needn't have worried.

For the next half hour, Robin was entertained with a series of riddles, nonsense rhymes and off-key renditions of Jeff's favorite songs from summer camp.

"Knock knock," she said when it appeared her son had run through his repertoire.

"Who's there?"

"Wanda."

"Wanda who?"

"Wanda who thinks up these silly jokes?"

Jeff laughed as though she'd come up with the funniest line ever devised. Her son's enthusiasm couldn't help but rub off on Robin and some of her weariness eased. Camping was fun—sort of. But it had been years since she'd slept on the ground and, frankly, she couldn't remember it being quite this hard.

"Do you think we'll be warm enough?" she teased. Jeff had used every blanket they owned, first to construct the tent and then to pad it. To be on the safe side, two or three more were piled on top of their sleeping bags on the off-chance an Arctic frost descended upon them. It was spring, but a San Francisco spring could be chilly.

"Sure," he answered, missing the kidding note in her voice. "But if you get cold, you can have one of mine."

"I'm fine," she assured him.

"You hungry?"

Now that she thought about it, she was. "Sure. Whatcha got?"

Jeff disappeared into his sleeping bag and returned a moment later with a limp package of licorice, a small plastic bag full of squashed marshmallows and a flattened box of raisins. Robin decided to forgo the snack.

"When are we going to buy me my dog?" Jeff asked, chewing loudly on the raisins.

Robin listened to the sound and said nothing.

"Mom...the dog?" he repeated after a few moments.

Robin had been dreading the question most of the day. She'd managed to forestall Jeff for the past month by telling him they'd discuss getting a dog after they were settled in their house.

"I thought we'd start looking for ads in the paper first thing tomorrow," Jeff said, still munching.

"I'm not sure when we'll start the search for the right dog." She was a coward, Robin freely admitted, but she so hated to disappoint Jeff. He had his heart set on a dog. How like his father he was, in his love for animals.

"I want a big one, you know. None of those fancy little poodles or anything."

"A collie would be nice, don't you think?"

"Or a German shepherd," Jeff added.

"Your father loved dogs," she whispered, although she'd told Jeff that countless times. Lonny had been gone for so many years, she had trouble remem-

bering what their lives had been like together. They'd
been crazy in love with each other and married shortly
after their high-school graduation. A year later, Robin
became pregnant. Jeff had been barely six months old
when Lonny was killed in a freak car accident on his
way home from work. In the span of a few short moments, Robin's comfortable cozy world had been sent
into a tailspin, and ten years later it was still whirling.

With her family's help, she'd gone back to school
and obtained her degree. She was now a Certified
Public Accountant working for a large San Francisco
insurance firm. Over the years she'd dated a number
of men, but none she'd ever seriously consider marrying. She wasn't a high-school kid any longer and her
life was far more complicated now than it had been at
eighteen. The thought of falling in love again terrified her.

"What kind of dog did Dad have when he was a
kid?" Jeff asked.

"I don't think Rover was any particular breed,"
Robin answered, then paused to recall exactly what
Lonny's childhood dog had looked like. "I think he
was mostly... Labrador."

"Was he black?"

"And brown."

"Did Dad keep any other animals?"

Robin smiled at the warm memory of her late husband. She enjoyed the way Jeff loved hearing stories
about his father. No matter how many times he'd
heard them. "He collected three more pets the first
year we were married. It seemed he was always bringing home a stray cat or lost dog. We couldn't keep
them, of course, because we weren't allowed pets in
the apartment complex. We went to great lengths to

hide them for a few days until we could locate their owners or find them a good home. For our first wedding anniversary, he bought me a goldfish. Your father really loved animals.''

Jeff beamed and planted his chin on top of his folded arms.

''We dreamed of buying a farm someday and raising chickens and pigs and maybe a cow or two. Your father even talked of buying a pony for you.'' Hard as she might try, she couldn't quite hide the pain in her voice. Even after all these years, the memory of Lonny's sudden death still hurt. Looking at her son, so eager for a dog of his own, Robin missed her husband more than ever.

''You and Dad were going to buy a farm?'' Jeff cried, his young voice ebullient. ''A pony for me? Really? Do you think we'll ever be able to afford one? Look how long it took to save enough to buy the house.''

Robin smiled. ''I think we'll have to give up on the idea of you and me owning a farm, at least in the near future.''

When they'd first married, Robin and Lonny had talked for hours about their dreams. They'd charted their lives, confident that nothing would ever separate them. Their love had been far too strong. Robin had never told Jeff about buying a farm. Nor had she told him how they'd planned to name it Paradise. Paradise, because that was what the farm would be to them. In retrospect, not telling Jeff was a way of protecting him. He'd lost so much—not only the guidance and love of his father but all the things they could have had as a family. She'd never mentioned the pony before, or the fact that Lonny had always longed for a horse of his own, too....

Jeff yawned loudly and Robin marveled at his endurance. He'd carted in as many boxes as the movers had, racing up and down the stairs with an energy Robin could only envy. He'd unpacked the upstairs bathroom, as well as his own bedroom and had helped her organize the kitchen.

"I can hardly wait to get my dog," Jeff said, his voice tapering to a murmur. Within minutes he was sound asleep.

"A dog," Robin said softly as her eyes closed. She didn't know how she was going to break the bad news to Jeff. They couldn't get a dog—at least not right away. She was unwilling to leave a large dog locked indoors all day while she went off to work and Jeff was in school. Tying one up in the backyard was equally unappealing, and she couldn't afford to build a fence. Not this year, anyway. Then there was the cost of feeding a dog and paying the vet bills. With this new home, Robin's budget was already stretched to the limit.

ROBIN AWOKE FEELING chilled and warm at the same time. In the gray dawn, she glanced at her watch. Six-thirty. At some point during the night, the old sleeping bag that dated back to her high-school days had come unzipped and the cool morning air had chilled her arms and legs. Yet her back was warm and cozy. Jeff had probably snuggled up to her during the night. She sighed, determined to go back to sleep for another half hour or so. With that thought in mind, she reached for a blanket to wrap around her shoulders and met with some resistance. She tugged and pulled, but to no avail. It was then that she felt something wet and warm close to her neck. Her eyes shot open. Very slowly, she turned her head until she came eyeball to eyeball with a big black dog.

Robin gasped loudly and struggled into a sitting position, which was difficult with the sleeping bag and several blankets wrapped around her legs, imprisoning her.

"Where did you come from?" she demanded, edging away from the dog. The Labrador had eased himself between her and Jeff and made himself right at home. His head rested on his paws and he looked perfectly content, if a bit disgruntled to have his nap interrupted. He didn't seem at all interested in vacating the premises.

Jeff rolled over and opened his eyes. Immediately, he bolted upright. "Mom," he cried excitedly. "You got me a dog!"

"No—he isn't ours. I don't know who he belongs to."

"Me!" Jeff's voice was triumphant. "He belongs to me." His thin arms hugged the animal's neck. "You really got me a dog! It was supposed to be a surprise, wasn't it?"

"Jeff," she said firmly. "I don't know where this animal came from, but he isn't ours."

"He isn't?" His voice sagged in disappointment. "But who owns him then? And how did he get inside the tent with us?"

"Heavens, I don't know." Robin rubbed the sleep from her eyes while she attempted to put her garbled thoughts in some kind of order. "He looks too well fed and groomed to be a stray. He must belong to someone in the neighborhood. Maybe he—"

"Blackie!" As if in reply, she was interrupted by a crisp male voice. "Blackie. Here, boy."

The Labrador lifted his head, but stayed where he was. Robin didn't blame him. Jeff was stroking his back with one hand and rubbing his ears with the other, all the while crooning to him softly.

With some effort, Robin managed to divest herself of the sleeping bag. She reached for her tennis shoes and crawled out of the tent. No sooner was she on her feet than she turned to find a lanky man standing not more than a few yards from her, just on the other side of the hedge that separated the two properties. Obviously he was her neighbor. Robin smiled, but the friendly gesture was not returned. In fact, the man looked downright *un*friendly.

Her neighbor was also an imposing man, at least six feet tall. Since Robin was only five-three, he towered head and shoulders above her. Instinctively, she stiffened her back, meeting his dark eyes. "Good morning," she said coolly.

He barely looked in her direction, and when he did, he dismissed her with little more than a nod. After a night on the ground, with her son and a dog for bedmates, Robin realized she wasn't going to win any beauty pageants, but she resented the way his eyes flickered disinterestedly over her.

Robin usually gave people the benefit of the doubt, but toward this man, she felt an immediate antipathy. His face was completely emotionless, which gave him an intimidating air. He was clearly aware of that and used it to his advantage.

"Good morning," she said again, clasping her hands tightly. She drew herself to her full height and lifted her chin. "I believe your dog is in the tent with my son."

Her news appeared to surprise him; his face softened. Robin was struck by the change. When his face relaxed, he was actually a very attractive man. For the most part, Robin barely noticed how good-looking a man was or wasn't, but this time . . . she noticed. Perhaps because of the contrast with his forbidding demeanor of only a moment before.

"Blackie knows better than to leave the yard. Here, boy!" He shouted for the Labrador again, this time including a sharp whistle loud enough to pierce Robin's eardrums. Almost immediately the dog emerged from the tent and reluctantly approached the hedge.

"Is that your dog?" Jeff asked, dashing out right behind Blackie. "He's great. How long have you had him?"

"I'll make sure he doesn't bother you again," the man said, ignoring Jeff's question. Robin supposed his words were meant to be an apology. "He's well trained—he's never left my yard before. I'll make sure it doesn't happen again."

"Blackie wasn't any bother," Jeff hurried to explain, racing forward. "He crawled into the tent with us and made himself at home, which was all right with us, wasn't it, Mom?"

"Sure," Robin answered, flipping her shoulder-length auburn hair away from her face. She'd had it tied at the nape when she'd gone to bed, but it had pulled free during the night. Robin could well imagine how it looked now. Most mornings it tended to resemble foam on a newly poured mug of beer.

"We're friends, aren't we, Blackie?" Jeff knelt, and without hesitation the dog came to him, eagerly licking his face.

The man's eyes revealed fleeting surprise, and his dark brows drew together over his high-bridged nose. "Blackie," he snapped. "Heel."

The Labrador squeezed between two overgrown laurel bushes and returned to his master, who didn't look any too pleased at his dog's affection for Jeff.

"My son has a way with animals," Robin explained.

"Do you live here?" Jeff asked next. He seemed completely unaware of their new neighbor's unfriendliness.

"Next door."

"Oh, good," Jeff returned with a wide grin. He placed his right hand on his chest. "I'm Jeff Masterson and this is my mom, Robin. We moved in yesterday."

"I'm Cole Camden. Welcome to the neighborhood."

Although his words were cordial, his tone wasn't. Nor the look on his face. Robin felt about as welcome as a punk-rock band at a retirees' picnic.

"I'm getting a dog myself soon," Jeff went on affably. "That's why we moved out of the apartment building—I couldn't have a pet there except my goldfish."

Cole nodded without comment.

Oh, great, Robin thought. After years of scrimping and saving to buy a house, they were going to be stuck with an ill-tempered next-door neighbor. His house was older than the others on the block. Much bigger, too. Robin guessed that his home, a sprawling three-story structure, was built in the early thirties. She knew that at one time this neighborhood had been filled with large opulent homes like Cole Camden's. Gradually, over the years, the older homes had been torn down and a series of two-story houses and trendy ramblers built in their place. Her neighbor's house was the last vestige of an era long past.

"Have you got any kids?" Jeff could hardly keep the eagerness out of his voice. In the apartment complex there had always been plenty of playmates around, and the ten-year-old was eager to make new friends, especially before he started classes in an unfamiliar school on Monday morning.

Cole's face hardened and Robin could have sworn the question had angered him. An uncomfortable moment passed before he answered. "No, I don't have any kids." His voice held a rough undertone, and for a split second Robin was sure she saw a flash of pain in his eyes.

"Would it be all right if I played with Blackie sometimes? Just until I got my own dog?"

"No." Cole's response was sharp, but when Jeff flinched at the vehemence with which he spoke, Cole appeared to regret his harsh tone. "I don't mean to be rude, but it would probably be best if you stayed in your own yard."

"That's all right," Jeff said. "You can send Blackie over here to visit any time you want. I like dogs."

"I can see that." A hint of a smile lifted the corners of his mouth. Then his cool gaze moved from Jeff to Robin, his face again expressionless, but she sensed that in some way he'd made up his mind about them, categorized them and come to his own conclusions.

If Cole Camden thought he could intimidate her, Robin had news for him. He'd broadcast his message loud and clear. He didn't want to be bothered by her or her son, and in return he'd stay out of her way. That was fine with her. Terrific, in fact. She didn't have time for humoring grouches.

Without another word, Cole turned and strode toward his house with Blackie at his heels.

"Goodbye, Mr. Camden," Jeff called, raising his hand.

Robin wasn't surprised when their neighbor didn't give them the courtesy of a reply.

In an effort to distract Jeff from Cole Camden's unfriendliness, she said brightly, "Hey, I'm starving. How about you?"

Jeff didn't answer right away. "Do you think he'll let me play with Blackie?"

Robin sighed, thinking about the dilemma that faced her. She didn't want Cole to hurt Jeff's feelings, but it wasn't likely their neighbor would appreciate her son's affinity with his Labrador. By the same token, a neighbor's dog, even one that belonged to a grouch, would ease her guilt over not being able to provide Jeff with the dog she'd promised him.

"What do you think, Mom?" Jeff prompted. "He'll probably let me play with Blackie sometimes, don't you think?"

"I don't know, honey," she whispered. "I just don't know."

LATER THE SAME DAY, after buying groceries to stock their bare kitchen shelves and picking up several other necessities, Robin counted the change at the bottom of her purse to be sure she had enough money for the subway Monday morning. Luckily she had enough spare change for BART—Bay Area Rapid Transit—for the week, but it was packed lunches for her and Jeff until payday, which was two weeks away.

Her finances would have been in better shape if they could have waited another year to move out of the apartment, but at the rate property values were rising, Robin couldn't possibly have saved to keep pace with inflation. The interest rates were at a two-year low and she'd decided soon after the first of the year that if she was ever going to move out of the apartment this was the time.

"Mom!" Jeff crashed through the back door, breathless. "We're in trouble."

"Oh?" Robin glanced up from the salad she was mixing. A completely disgusted look on his face, her son flung himself into a chair and plopped his elbows on the table. Then he let out a forceful sigh.

"What's wrong, Jeff?"

"I'm afraid we made a bad mistake."

"How's that?"

"There're nothing but girls in this neighborhood." He made it sound as though they'd unexpectedly landed in enemy territory. "I rode my bike up and down the street and all I saw were girls." He wrinkled his nose with aversion.

"Don't worry, you'll be meeting lots of boys in school Monday."

"You aren't taking this seriously!" Jeff cried. "I don't even think you fully understand what this means. There are seven houses on this block. Six of them have kids and only one has a boy, and that's me. I'm surrounded by women!"

"How'd you find all this out?"

"I asked, of course." He sighed again. "What are you going to do about it, Mom?"

"Me?" Robin asked, somewhat taken aback. "Are you suggesting we move back to the apartment?"

Jeff considered this for only a moment. "I'd think we should if it weren't for two things. We can't have a dog there. And I found a fort."

"A fort?"

"Yes," he said solemnly. "It's hidden way back in Mr. Camden's yard and covered by a bunch of brush. It's real neat there. I don't think he knows about it, because the word on the street is he doesn't like kids. Someone must have built it and I'm going to find out who. If there's a club going, I want in. I've got the right—I live closer to Mr. Camden than anyone else does."

"Agreed." Robin munched on a slice of green pepper and handed one to Jeff. "So you think it would be all right if we stayed?"

"I guess so," Jeff conceded, "at least until I find out more about the fort."

Robin was about to say something else when the doorbell chimed.

Jeff's blue eyes met hers. "I bet it's one of those pesky girls," he said in disgust.

"Do you want me to get rid of her?"

Jeff nodded emphatically. "Please."

Robin was smiling when she answered the front door. Jeff was right about one thing—it was a girl, and one who, she guessed, was a couple of years younger than her son. She hadn't come alone, though. Standing with the youngster was an adult.

"Hi," the woman said cheerfully, flashing Robin a warm smile. "I know you've barely had a chance to get settled in, but I wanted to introduce myself. I'm Heather Lawrence and this is my daughter, Kelly. We live next door, and we'd like to welcome you to the neighborhood."

Robin introduced herself as she opened the door and invited them in. Heather was cute and perky. Her hair was cut in a short bob that bounced when she spoke. Robin knew right away she was going to like her neighbor. Heather's warm reception was a pleasant change from the way Cole Camden had welcomed her.

"Would you like some coffee?" Robin asked.

"If you're sure I'm not interrupting anything."

"I'm sure." Robin led the way into the kitchen where Jeff sat waiting. He cast her a look that suggested she should be shot for treason, then muttered something about forgetting that mothers were really *girls* in disguise and headed out the front door.

Robin reached for two matching ceramic mugs and poured a cup of coffee for her new friend. She offered Kelly a glass of juice, then slid into the chair across the table from the girl and her mother. "I'm sorry about Jeff." She felt obliged to apologize. "He's at the age where he thinks girls are a plague to society."

"Don't worry about it," Heather said, smiling. "Kelly isn't keen on boys herself."

"They're creeps. I'd rather ride my bicycle than visit with a boy, anyway," the girl announced. "But Mom wanted me to come over here with her so she didn't look like a busybody. Right, Mom?"

Heather blushed and cast her daughter a murderous glance.

Robin laughed. "I thought it would take several weeks to get to know my neighbors and I've met two in one day."

"Someone else has already been over?"

"Cole Camden introduced himself this morning," she explained, keeping her eyes averted to hide the resentment she felt toward her unfriendly neighbor. Even now, hours later, she couldn't help thinking about the way he'd reacted to her and Jeff.

"Cole Camden introduced himself?" Heather repeated, sounding shocked. She frowned, staring into space as though digesting the fact.

"To be honest, I think he would have preferred to avoid me until the next Ice Age, but his dog wanted to make friends with Jeff."

Heather's mouth opened and closed twice. "Blackie did?"

"Is there something strange about that?"

"Frankly, yes. To say Cole keeps to himself is an understatement. I don't think he's said more than a handful of words to me in the entire two years since Kelly and I moved here. I don't know why he continues to live in the neighborhood." She paused to respond to her daughter, who was asking permission to go back home. "Thank Robin for the juice, honey. Anyway," she went on, turning back to Robin when her daughter skipped out the door, "he's all alone in that huge house and it's ridiculous, really. Can you imagine what his heating bills must be? Although personally, I don't think money is much of a problem for him. But then, that's something I wouldn't know."

It didn't surprise Robin to learn Cole lived alone. She'd barely met the man, but guessed that life held little joy for him. It was as though love, warmth and friendship had all been found lacking and had therefore been systematically dismissed.

"Apparently, he was married once. At least that's what I've heard, but he was divorced long before I moved here."

Robin had dealt with unfriendly men before, but something about Cole struck her hard and deep, and she wasn't sure what it was or why he would evoke such a strong feeling within her.

"He and his dog are inseparable," Heather added.

Robin nodded, barely listening. He'd intimidated her at first, but when she'd pulled herself together and faced him squarely, he'd loosened up a bit and, later, even seemed amused. But then Jeff had asked him about children, and Robin had witnessed the flash of pain in his eyes.

As if by magic, her son's face appeared around the door. When he saw that Kelly was gone, he walked into the room, hands buried in his back pockets.

"Do you have a dog?" he asked Heather.

"Unfortunately, no. Kelly's allergic to animal fur."

Jeff nodded as though to say that was exactly the kind of thing he expected from a girl. "We're getting a German shepherd soon, aren't we, Mom?"

"Soon," Robin responded, feeling wretched. After Heather left, she was going to tell Jeff the truth. She fully intended to let him have his dog, but he'd have to wait a while. For a good part of the day, she'd been practicing what to say. She'd even come up with a compromise idea. They could get a cat. Cats didn't seem to mind being left on their own, and they didn't need the same kind of exercise. Although she wasn't crazy about keeping a litter box in the house, Robin was willing to put up with that inconvenience until she could afford to have a fence built. She planned to be positive and direct with Jeff. He'd understand. At least she hoped he would.

Heather stayed only a few minutes more, and the visit was a fruitful one. Robin learned that Heather was divorced, worked mornings in an office, and provided after-school day care in an effort to spend more time with Kelly. This information was good news to Robin and the two women agreed that Jeff would go to the Lawrence house before and after school, instead of the community center several blocks away. The arrangement suited them both; even Jeff shrugged his agreement.

Robin would have liked to ask her new friend more about Cole, but his name didn't come up again, and she didn't want to seem too curious about him.

After Heather left, Robin braced herself for the talk with Jeff about getting a dog. Unfortunately, it didn't go well. It seemed that after waiting nearly ten years, a few more months was completely unacceptable.

"You promised!" he shouted. "You said I could have a dog when we moved into the house!"

"You can, sweetheart, but not right away."

Unusual for Jeff, tears gathered in his eyes, and he struggled to hold them back. Soon Robin felt moisture filling her own eyes. She hated disappointing Jeff more than anything. His heart was set on getting a dog right away, and he considered the offer of a cat a poor substitute.

He left the house soon afterward. In an effort to soothe his hurt feelings, Robin cooked her son's favorite meal—macaroni and cheese with sliced wieners and lots of ketchup.

She didn't see him on the sidewalk or the street when she went to check a half hour later. She stood on the porch, wondering where he'd gone. His bike was parked inside the garage, and he'd already aired his views about playing with any of the girls in the neighborhood.

It would be just like him to storm into his room in a fit of indignation and promptly fall asleep. Robin hurried upstairs to his bedroom, which was across the hall from her own.

His bed was made and his clothes hung neatly in the closet. Robin decided that in another day or two, everything would be back to normal.

It wasn't until she turned to leave that she saw the note on his desk. Picking it up, Robin read the first line. Immediately, she felt a swirling sense of panic.

Dear Mom,
You broke your promise. You said I could have a dog and now you say I have to wait. If I can't have a dog, then I don't want to live with you anymore. This is goodbye forever.

Love, Jeff

CHAPTER TWO

FOR A MOMENT, Robin was too stunned to react. Her heart was pounding so hard it echoed in her ears like thunder, so loud it seemed to knock her off balance.

Rushing down the stairs, she stood on the porch, cupped her hands over her mouth and screamed frantically. "Jeff!"

Cole Camden was standing on his front porch, too. He released a shrill whistle and stood waiting expectantly. When nothing happened, he called, "Blackie!"

"Jeff!" Robin tried again.

"Blackie!"

Robin called for Jeff once more, but her voice cracked as the panic engulfed her. She paused, placed her hand over her mouth and closed her eyes in an effort to gather her composure, which was crumbling more every minute.

"Blackie!" Cole yelled. He looked furious about his dog's disappearance.

It took Robin only a moment to put two and two together. "Cole," she cried, running across the lawn toward him, "I think Jeff and Blackie might have run away together."

Cole looked at her as though she were deranged, and Robin couldn't really blame him. "Jeff left me a note. He wants a dog so badly and we can't get one right away because...well, because we can't, and I had to tell him, and he was terribly disappointed and he decided to run away.''

Cole's mouth thinned. ''The whole idea is ridiculous. Even if Jeff did run away, Blackie would never go with him.''

''Do you honestly think I'd make something like this up?'' she shrieked. ''The last time I saw Jeff was around four-thirty, and I'd bet cold cash that's about the same time Blackie disappeared.''

Cole's gaze narrowed. ''Then where are they?''

''If I knew that, do you think I'd be standing around here arguing with you?''

''Listen, lady, I don't know your son, but I know my dog and—''

''My name's not lady,'' Robin flared, clenching her hands into tight fists at her sides. He was looking at her as though she were a madwoman on the loose—which she was where her son was concerned. ''I'm sorry to have troubled you. When I find Jeff, I'll see to it that your dog finds his way home.''

Cole's eyes shot sparks in her direction, but she ignored them. Turning abruptly, she ran back to her own house. Halfway there, she stopped dead, and whirled around to face Cole again. ''The fort.''

''What fort?'' Cole demanded.

''The one that's back in the farthest corner of your yard. It's covered with brush.... Jeff found it earlier today. He wouldn't know anywhere to go and that would be the perfect hiding place.''

''No one's been there in years,'' Cole said, discounting her suggestion.

''The least we can do is look.''

Cole's nod was reluctant. He led the way to his backyard, which was much larger than hers. There was

a small grove of oak trees at the rear of the property
and beyond that a high fence. Apparently the fort was
situated between the trees and the fence. A few minutes later, in the most remote corner of the yard, nes-
tled between two trees, Robin spied the small wooden
structure, which blended into the terrain. If Robin
hadn't been looking for the hideaway, she'd never have
seen it.

It was obvious when they neared the space that
someone had taken up residence. Cole lowered himself onto all fours, peered inside, then looked back at
Robin with a nod. He breathed in sharply, apparently
irritated by this turn of events, and agilely crawled
through the narrow entrance.

Not about to be left standing by herself, Robin got
down on her knees and followed him in.

Just as she'd suspected, Jeff and Blackie were hud-
dled together in a corner. Jeff was sound asleep and
Blackie was curled up at his side, guarding him. When
Cole and Robin entered, the Labrador lifted his head
and wagged his tail in greeting.

The fort wasn't much bigger than the tent Jeff had
constructed the night before, and Robin was forced to
pull her knees close and loop her arms around them.
Cole's larger body seemed to fill every available bit of
space.

Jeff must have sensed that his newfound home had
been invaded because his eyes fluttered open and he
gazed at Robin, then twisted his head to stare at Cole.

"Hi, Mom," he said sheepishly. "I bet I'm in trouble, aren't I?"

Robin was so grateful to find him, all she could do
was nod. If she'd tried to speak, her voice would have

wobbled and heaved with emotion, which would only have embarrassed them both.

"So, Jeff," Cole said sternly. "You were going to run away from home. I see you brought everything you needed with you." He pushed the frying pan and atlas into the middle of their cramped quarters. "What I want to know is how you convinced Blackie to join you."

"He came all on his own. He just sort of followed me," Jeff murmured, but his eyes avoided Cole's. "I wouldn't have taken him on purpose—he's your dog."

"I'm glad you didn't . . . coerce him."

"All you took was a frying pan and an atlas!" Robin cried, staring at the cast-iron skillet and the atlas with its dog-eared pages.

Cole and Jeff both ignored her outburst.

"I take it you don't like living around here?" Cole asked.

Jeff stiffened, then vigorously shook his head. "Mom told me when we moved I could have a dog and now I can't, and worse than that she dragged me into a neighborhood filled with girls. That would have been all right if I had a dog, but then she broke her promise. A promise is a promise and it's sacred. A guy would never do that."

"So you can't have the dog until later?"

"And all because of a stupid fence."

Cole nodded. "Fences are important, you know. You know what else? Your mom was worried about you."

Jeff looked at Robin, who was blinking furiously to keep the tears from dripping down her face. The upheaval and stress of the move had drained her emotionally and she was an unmitigated mess. Normally, she was a calm, controlled person, but this whole thing with Jeff was her undoing. That and the fact she'd hardly slept the night before in the makeshift tent.

"Mom," Jeff said, studying her anxiously, "are you all right?"

She covered her face with both hands. "I slept with a dog and you ran away and all you took was a frying pan and an atlas." That made no sense whatsoever. Robin felt as if she'd been run over by a steamroller, and once the tears started, they wouldn't stop. Her shoulders shook jerkily.

"I'm sorry, Mom," Jeff said softly. "I didn't mean to make you cry."

"I know," she whimpered. "I want you to have a dog, I really do, but we can't keep one locked up in a house all day and we don't have a fence and...and you looked at me and I swear it was Lonny all over again."

"Who's Lonny?" Cole cocked his head toward Jeff, speaking in a whisper.

"Lonny was my dad. He died when I was real little. I don't even remember him."

Cole shared a knowing look with her son. "It might be a good idea if we got your mother inside the house."

"You think I'm getting hysterical, don't you?" Robin cried. "I want you both to know I'm in perfect control. A woman can cry every now and again if she wants. Venting your emotions is healthy—all those books say so."

"Right, Mom." Jeff gently patted her shoulder, then crawled out of the fort. He waited for Robin, who emerged after him, and offered her a hand. Cole and Blackie followed.

Jeff took Robin's arm, cupping her elbow as he led her toward the back door of their house, as if he suspected she couldn't find her way without his guidance.

Once inside, Robin reached for a tissue and loudly blew her nose. Her composure was shaky, but when she turned to Cole, she intended to be as reasonable as a judge. As polite as a preacher.

"Have you got any aspirin?" Cole asked Jeff.

Jeff nodded, and dashed up the stairs to the bathroom, returning in thirty seconds flat with the bottle. Cole filled a glass with water and delivered both to Robin. How he knew she had a fierce headache, she could only guess.

"Why don't you lie down for a couple of minutes? I'm sure you'll feel better."

"I feel just fine, thank you," she snapped, more angry with herself for overreacting than with him for taking charge.

"Do you have family close by?" Again Cole directed the question to Jeff, which only served to further infuriate Robin. Jeff was ten years old! She, on the other hand, was the adult. If this man had questions they should be directed to her, not her son.

"Not anymore," Jeff answered in an anxious whisper. "Grandma and Grandpa moved to Arizona last year, and my uncle lives in L.A."

"I don't need to lie down," Robin said forcefully. "I'm perfectly fine."

"Mom," Jeff countered, his voice troubled, "you don't look so good."

"You were talking about frying pans and sleeping with dogs in the same breath," Cole elaborated, his eyebrows raised.

"I think Mr. Camden's right," Jeff concurred. "You need rest—lots of rest."

Her own son had turned traitor on her. Robin couldn't believe it. Jeff took her hand gently and led her into the family room, which was directly off the kitchen. He patted the quilted pillow on the sofa, wordlessly suggesting she place her head there. When she resisted, he pulled the afghan from the chair and draped it around her, securely tucking the ends behind her shoulders, as though she were in imminent danger of freezing to death.

Robin couldn't believe she was allowing herself to be led around like a . . . like a puppy. As if reading her thoughts, Blackie wandered over to her side and lowered his bulk onto the carpet beside the sofa.

"That's a neat fort you've got there," Jeff told Cole once he'd finished tucking in the blanket. Robin watched him hurry back to the kitchen, grab a plate, then load it with macaroni and cheese and hand it to Cole, apparently wanting to share his favorite meal with their neighbor.

Cole set the plate on the counter. "Thanks anyway, Jeff, but I've got to get back to the house. In the future, if you're thinking about running away—don't."

"Yeah, I guess you're right," Jeff said with a mildly guilty look. "My mom turned into a basket case."

Cole smiled—at least, it was as close to a smile as Robin had seen. "You're both going to be all right. She intends to get you that dog, you know. Just hang on, it'll be sooner than you think."

Jeff walked to the sliding glass door with Cole. "Mr. Camden, can I ask you something important?"

"Sure." He stood just inside the house.

"Is anyone using the fort?"

"Not that I know of."

Jeff looked hopeful. "It didn't look like anyone had been inside for a long time."

"Six years," Cole murmured absently.

"That long? How come?" Jeff asked. "It's a great fort. If it's all right with you I'd like to go over there sometimes. I promise not to walk in any flower beds or anything, and I won't leave a mess. I'll take real good care of everything."

Cole hesitated only for a moment. He looked at Jeff, and Robin held her breath as his expression softened. Then he shook his head. "Maybe sometime in the future, but not now."

Jeff's deep blue eyes brightened; apparently the refusal didn't trouble him. "That's great. When I can use the fort, would it be all right if I took Blackie with me? He followed me today, you know. I didn't have to do anything to get him to tag along." Jeff paused and lowered his eyes. "Well, hardly anything."

"I thought as much. As your mom said, you have a way with animals."

"My dad did, too. If he hadn't died he would have gotten me a pony and everything."

There was such pride in Jeff's voice that Robin bit her bottom lip to keep from crying all over again. Jeff and Lonny were so much alike. What she'd said to her son earlier had been true. More and more, Jeff was starting to take on his father's looks and personality.

Cole hesitated, gazing down at Jeff. An emotion flashed in his eyes, so transient Robin couldn't name it. He laid his hand on Jeff's thin shoulder. "Since your mother explained there's going to be a delay in getting you a dog, it'd be all right to borrow Blackie every now and then. As long as you stay in your own yard. I don't want him running in the neighborhood unless he's on a leash."

"Do you really mean it? Gee, thanks, Mr. Camden. I'll do everything you ask."

Robin had the feeling Jeff would have agreed to just about any terms as long as he could see Blackie. It wasn't a dog of his own, but it was as close as he was going to get for the next few months.

Once Cole had left, Jeff joined her on the sofa, his hands folded together on his lap. "I'm sorry, Mom," he muttered, his chin buried in his chest. "I promise I'll never run away again."

"I should hope not," she said. Wrapping her arms around him, she hugged him close, kissing his cheek.

"Gee whiz," Jeff grumbled, rubbing his face. "I'd never have apologized if I'd known you were going to kiss me."

A WEEK PASSED. Jeff liked his new school and, as Robin had predicted, he found his class contained an equal number of boys and girls. With his outgoing personality, he quickly collected a handful of new friends.

On Sunday afternoon, Robin was in the family room reading the newspaper when Jeff ambled in and sat down across the room from her. He took the baseball cap from his head and studied it for several moments.

"Something bothering you?" she asked, lowering the paper to get a better view of her son.

He shrugged. "Did you know Mr. Camden used to be married?"

"I heard something along those lines," Robin said absently. But other than Heather's remarks the previous week, she hadn't learned anything else. In fact, she'd spoken to her neighbor only when she went to pick Jeff up every afternoon. The child-care arrangement with Heather was working beautifully, but there had been little opportunity to chat.

As for Cole, Robin hadn't seen him at all. Since he'd been so kind and helpful in the situation with Jeff, Robin had revised her opinion of him. He liked his privacy and that was fine by her; she had no intention of interrupting his serene existence. The memory of their first meeting still rankled, but she was willing to overlook that shaky beginning.

"Mr. Camden had a son who died."

Robin's heart constricted. It made sense: the flash of pain she'd seen when Jeff had asked him about children, the word on the street that Cole didn't like kids, the abandoned fort. "I... How did you find that out?"

"Jimmy Wallach. He lives two streets over and has an older brother who used to play with Bobby Camden. Jimmy told me about him."

"I didn't know," Robin murmured, saddened by the information. She couldn't imagine her life without Jeff—the mere thought of losing him was enough to tear her apart.

"Mrs. Wallach heard Jimmy talking about Bobby Camden and she said that Mr. Camden got divorced and it was real bad, and then a year or so later Bobby died. She said he's never been the same since. Like someone else took over his mind and body."

Robin ached for Cole, and she regretted all the uncharitable thoughts she'd had that first morning.

"I feel sad," Jeff whispered, frowning. His young face was as intent as she'd ever seen it.

"I do, too," Robin returned softly.

"Mrs. Wallach seemed real surprised when I told her Mr. Camden said I could play in Bobby's fort some day. Ever since his son died, he hasn't let any kids in the yard or anything. She said he hardly talks to anyone in the neighborhood anymore."

Heather Lawrence had said basically the same thing, but not the reason for it. Probably because she didn't know.

"Are you still going to barbecue hamburgers tonight for dinner?"

Robin nodded, surprised by the abrupt way Jeff had changed the subject. "If you want." Next to macaroni and cheese, grilled burgers were Jeff's all-time favorite food.

"Would it be all right if I invited Mr. Camden over to eat with us?"

Robin hated to refuse her son, but she wasn't sure a dinner invitation was a good idea. She didn't know Cole very well, but from what she'd learned he wasn't one to socialize with the neighbors. In addition, Jeff might blurt out questions about Cole's dead son that would be terribly painful for him.

"Mom," Jeff pleaded, "I bet no one ever invites him to dinner and he's all alone."

"Sweetheart, I don't know if that would be the right thing to do."

"But we owe him, Mom," Jeff implored. "He let me throw sticks for Blackie twice this week."

"I don't think Mr. Camden's home," Robin said, picking up the newspaper while she weighed the pros and cons of Jeff's suggestion. Since last Sunday, Robin hadn't spoken to Cole once, and she wasn't eager to initiate a conversation. He might read something into it.

"I'll go check and see if he's home." Before she could react, Jeff was out the front door, letting the screen door slam in his wake.

He returned a couple of minutes later breathless and excited. "Mr. Camden's home and he said he appreciated the invitation, but he had other plans for tonight."

"That's too bad," Robin murmured, hoping she sounded sincere.

"I told him we were having strawberry shortcake for dessert and he said that was his favorite."

Robin hated to admit it, but she was relieved Cole wouldn't be showing up for dinner. The man made her feel nervous and uncertain. She didn't know why that should be, only that it was a new and unfamiliar sensation.

"Thanks, Mom."

Robin jerked her head up from the newspaper. "Thanks for what?" She hadn't read a word in five minutes. Her thoughts had been dominated by her neighbor.

Jeff rolled his eyes. "For letting me take a piece of strawberry shortcake over to Mr. Camden."

"I said you could do that?"

"Just now." He walked over to her and playfully tested her forehead with the back of his hand. "You don't feel hot, but then, with brain fever you never know."

Robin swatted playfully at her son's backside.

Laughing, Jeff raced outdoors, where his bicycle was waiting. A half hour later, he was back in the house. "Mom! Mom!" he cried, racing into the kitchen. "Did you know Mr. Camden owns a black Porsche?"

"I can't say I did." She was more interested in peeling potatoes for the salad than discussing fancy cars. She didn't know enough about sports cars to get excited about them.

Jeff jerked open the bottom drawer and rooted through the rag bag until he found what he was looking for. He pulled out a large square that had once been part of his flannel pajamas, then started back outside. "He has another car too, a big four-wheel drive."

"Just where are you going, young man?" Robin demanded.

"Mr. Camden's waxing his car and I thought I'd go help him."

"Did he ask for your help?"

"No," Jeff said impatiently.

"He may not want you to."

"Mom!" Jeff rolled his eyes as if to suggest she was overdoing this mothering thing. "Can I go now?"

"Ah... I suppose," she agreed, but her heart was in her throat. She moved into the living room and watched as Jeff strolled across the lawn to the driveway where Cole was busy rubbing liquid wax on the gleaming surface of his Porsche. Without a word, Jeff started polishing the dried wax with his rag. Cole straightened and stopped smearing on the wax, obviously surprised to see Jeff. Robin bit her lower lip, not knowing how her neighbor would react to Jeff's willingness to help. Apparently he said something, because Jeff nodded, then walked over and sat cross-legged on the lawn. They didn't seem to be carrying on a conversation and Robin couldn't help wondering what Cole had said to her son.

Robin returned to the kitchen, grateful that Cole's rejection had apparently been gentle. At least he hadn't sent Jeff away. She peeled another potato, then walked back into the living room and glanced out the window again. This time she discovered Jeff standing next to Cole, who was, it seemed, demonstrating the right way to polish a car. He made wide circular motions with his arms, then stepped aside to let Jeff tackle the Porsche again. Cole nodded and smiled, then patted him on the head before walking around to the other side of the car.

Once the salad was ready, Robin decided to venture outside.

Jeff paused and waved enthusiastically when he caught sight of her on the porch. "Isn't she a beaut?" he yelled.

It looked like an ordinary car to Robin, but she nodded enthusiastically. "Wonderful," she answered. "Afternoon, Cole."

"Robin." He returned her greeting absently.

He wore a sleeveless gray sweatshirt and she was surprised by how muscular and tanned his arms were. From her conversation with Heather Lawrence, Robin had learned Cole was a prominent attorney. And he'd seemed to fit the lawyer image to a T. Not anymore. The lawyer was gone and the *man* was there, bold as could be. Her awareness of him as an attractive virile male was shockingly intense.

The problem, she decided, lay in the fact that she hadn't expected Cole to look so... fit. The sight of all that lean muscle came as a pleasant surprise. Cole's

aggressive unfriendly expression had been softened as
he bantered teasingly with Jeff.

Blackie ambled to her side and Robin leaned over to
scratch the dog's ears while she continued to study his
master. Cole's hair was dark and grew away from his
brow, but a single lock flopped stubbornly over his
forehead and he had to toss it back from his face every
once in a while. It was funny how she'd never noticed
that about him until now.

Jeff must have said something humorous because
Cole threw back his head and chuckled loudly. It was
the first time she'd ever heard him laugh. She suspected he didn't often give in to the impulse. A smile
crowded Robin's face as Jeff started laughing, too.

In that moment the oddest thing happened. Robin
felt something catch in her heart. The tug was almost
physical, and she experienced a completely unfamiliar feeling of vulnerability....

"Do you need me to roll out the barbecue for you?"
Jeff shouted when he noticed she was still on the
porch. He'd turned his baseball cap around so that the
bill faced backward. While he spoke, his arm continued to work feverishly, buffing the passenger door
with his rag.

"Not . . . yet."

"Good, 'cause Mr. Camden needs me to finish up
this side for him. We're on a tight schedule here, and
I don't really have time. Cole's got a dinner date at
five-thirty."

"I see." Standing on the porch, dressed in her old
faded jeans, with a mustard-spotted terry-cloth hand
towel tucked in the waistband, Robin felt as appealing as Ma Kettle. "Any time you're finished is fine."

So Cole Camden's got a date, Robin mused. *Of course he's got a date,* she told herself. Why should she care? And if watching Jeff and Cole together was going to affect her like this, it would be best to go back into the house now.

Over dinner, all Jeff could talk about was Cole Camden. Every other sentence was Cole this and Cole that, until Robin was ready to slam her fist on the table and demand Jeff never mention their neighbor's name again.

"And the best part is, he paid me for helping him wax his car for him," Jeff continued, then stuffed the hamburger into his mouth, chewing a mile a minute in his enthusiasm.

"That was more than generous of him."

Jeff nodded enthusiastically. "Be sure and save some shortcake for him. He said not to bring it over 'cause he didn't know exactly when he'd get home. He'll stop by," he said.

"I will." Robin sincerely doubted her neighbor would. Jeff seemed to be under the impression Cole would show up at any time; Robin knew better. If Cole had a dinner date, he wasn't going to rush back just to taste her homemade dessert, though she did have to admit she made an excellent shortcake.

As she suspected, Cole didn't come by. Jeff grumbled about it the next morning. He was convinced Cole would have if Robin hadn't insisted Jeff go to bed at his regular time.

"I'll make shortcake again soon," Robin promised, hurrying to pack their lunches. "When I do, you can take a piece over to him."

"All right," Jeff muttered.

That evening, when Robin returned home from work, she found Jeff playing with Blackie in Cole's backyard.

"Jeff," she cried, alarmed that Cole might discover her son on his property. He'd made it clear Jeff wasn't to go into his yard. "What are you doing at Mr. Camden's? And why aren't you at Heather's?" She walked over to the hedge and placed her hands on her hips, frustrated with her ten-year-old.

"Blackie's chain got all tangled up," Jeff explained, looking sheepish. "He needed my help. I told Heather it would be okay with you and . . ." His voice trailed off.

"He's untangled now," Robin pointed out.

"I know, but since I was here it seemed like a good time for the two of us to—"

"Play," Robin completed for him.

"Yeah," her son said, nodding eagerly. Jeff was well aware he'd done wrong, but had difficulty admitting it.

"Mr. Camden doesn't want you in his yard, and we both know it." Standing next to the thick laurel hedge, Robin watched with dismay as Cole opened his back door and stepped outside. Blackie barked in greeting, and his tail swung with enough force to knock Jeff off balance.

When Cole noticed Jeff in his yard, he frowned and cast an accusing glare in Robin's direction.

"Jeff said Blackie's chain was tangled," she rushed to explain.

"How'd you get over here?" Cole asked her son, and although he didn't raise his voice, it was clear he was displeased. "The gate's locked and the hedge is too high to leap over."

Jeff stared down at the lawn. "I came through the gap in the hedge—the same one Blackie uses. I crawled through it."

"Was his chain really tangled?"

"No, sir," Jeff said in a voice so low Robin had to strain to hear him. "At least not much. He could have straightened it out himself.... I just thought, you know, that maybe he'd like the company."

"I see."

"He was all alone and so was I." Jeff lifted his eyes defiantly to his mother's, as if to suggest the fault was entirely hers. "I go to Mrs. Lawrence's after school, but it's all girls there, and I'd rather be shot than play with dolls."

"Don't you remember what I said about your coming into my yard?" Cole asked him.

Jeff nod was sluggish. "Yes. You said maybe I could sometime, but not now. I thought ... I hoped that since you let me help you wax your car you wouldn't mind so much."

"I mind," Cole said flatly.

"He won't do it again," Robin promised, "will you, Jeff?"

"No," he murmured. "I'm sorry, Mr. Camden."

For an entire week Jeff kept his word. The following Monday, however, when Robin returned from the BART station, Heather explained that Jeff had mysteriously disappeared about a half hour earlier. She assumed he'd gone home; he'd said something about expecting a call.

Unfortunately, Robin knew exactly where to look for him, and it wasn't at home. Even more unfortunate was the fact that Cole's car pulled into the driveway just as she was opening her door. Throwing aside her briefcase and purse, she rushed through the house, jerked open the sliding glass door at the back and raced across her yard.

Her son was nowhere to be seen, but she immediately realized he'd been with Blackie. The dog wasn't in evidence, and she could see Jeff's favorite baseball cap on the lawn.

"Jeff," she called, afraid to raise her voice. She sounded as though she was suffering from a bad case of laryngitis.

Neither boy nor dog appeared.

She tried again, taking the risk of shouting for Jeff in a normal tone, praying it wouldn't attract Cole's attention. No response. Since Jeff and Blackie didn't seem to be within earshot, she guessed they were in the fort. There was no help for it; she'd have to go after him herself. Her only hope was that she could hurry over to the fort, get Jeff and return to her own yard, all without being detected by Cole.

Finding the hole in the laurel proved difficult enough. The space was little more than a narrow gap between two thick plants, and for a distressing moment, Robin doubted she was slim enough to squeeze through. Finally, she lowered herself to the ground, hunched her shoulders and managed to push her way between the shrubs. Her head had just emerged when she noticed a pair of polished men's shoes on the other side. Slowly, reluctantly, she glanced up to find Cole towering above her, eyes narrowed with suspicion.

"Oh, hi," she said, striving to sound as though it was perfectly normal for her to be crawling into his yard on her hands and knees. "I suppose you're wondering exactly what I'm doing here...."

"The question did cross my mind."

CHAPTER THREE

"IT WAS THE MOST embarrassing moment of my entire life," Robin repeated for the third time. She was sitting at the kitchen table, resisting the urge to bury her face in her hands and weep.

"You've already said that," Jeff grumbled.

"What possessed you to even think about going into Mr. Camden's yard again? Honestly, Jeff, you've been warned not to at least half a dozen times. What do I have to do? String barbed wire between our yards?"

Although he'd thoroughly disgraced himself, Jeff casually rotated the rim of his baseball cap between his fingers. "I said I was sorry."

A mere apology in no way compensated for the humiliation Robin had suffered when Cole had found her down on all fours, crawling through his laurel hedge. If she lived to be an old woman, she would never forget the look on his face.

"You put me on television and phone restriction already," her son reminded her.

The punishment could be another mistake to add to her growing list. At times like this, she wished Lonny were there to advise her. She needed him, and even after all these years, still missed him. Often, when there wasn't anyone else around, Robin found herself talking to Lonny, discussing things. Without television and the phone, the most attractive form of entertainment left open to her son was playing with Blackie, which was what had got him into trouble in the first place.

"Blackie belongs to Mr. Camden," Robin felt obliged to tell him. Again.

"I know," Jeff said, "but he likes me. When I come home from school, he goes crazy. He's real glad to see me, and since there aren't a whole lot of boys in this neighborhood—" he paused as if she were to blame for that "—and Blackie and I have this understanding. We're buds."

"That's all fine and dandy, but you seem to be forgetting that Blackie doesn't belong to you." Robin stood and opened the refrigerator, taking out a package of chicken breasts.

"I wish he was my dog," Jeff grumbled. In an apparent effort to make peace, her son walked over to the cupboard, removed two plates and proceeded to set the table.

After dinner, while Robin was doing the dishes, the doorbell chimed. Jeff raced down the hallway to answer it even before Robin could dry her hands. Her son returned a moment later with Cole Camden at his side.

Her neighbor was the last person Robin had expected to see—and the last person she *wanted* to see.

"Mom," Jeff said, nodding toward Cole, "it's Mr. Camden."

"Hello, again," she managed, striving for a light tone, and realizing even as she spoke that she'd failed. "Would you like a cup of coffee?"

"No, thanks. I'd like to talk to both of you about—"

Not giving him the opportunity to continue, Robin nodded so hard and fast she nearly dislocated her neck. "I really am sorry about what happened. I've had a good long talk with Jeff and, frankly, I understand why you're upset and I don't blame you in the least. You've been more than understanding about this whole unfortunate episode and I want you to know there won't be a repeat performance of what happened today."

"From either of you?"

"Absolutely," she said, knowing her cheeks were as red as her fingernail polish. Did he have to remind her of the humiliating position he'd found her in earlier?

"Mom put me on television and phone restriction for an entire week," Jeff explained sheepishly. "I promise not to go into your fort again, Mr. Camden. And I promise not to go in my backyard after school, either, because Blackie sees me and gets all happy and excited—and I guess I get all happy and excited, too— and that's when I do what I'm not supposed to do."

"I see." Cole smiled down at Jeff. Robin found it a rather unusual smile. It didn't come from his lips so much as his eyes. Once more she witnessed a flash of pain, and another emotion she could only describe as longing. Slowly his gaze drifted to Robin. When his dark eyes met hers, she suddenly found herself short of breath.

"Actually I didn't come here to talk to you about what happened earlier this afternoon," Cole explained. "I'm going to be out of town for the next couple of days, and since Jeff and Blackie seem to get along so well, I thought Jeff might be willing to look after him. That way I won't have to put him in the kennel. Naturally I'm prepared to pay your son for his time and effort. If he'll agree, I'll let him play in the fort while I'm away."

Jeff's eyes grew rounder than Robin could ever remember seeing them. "You want me to watch Blackie?" he asked, his voice incredulous. "And you're going to *pay* me? Can Blackie spend the night here? Please?"

"I guess that answers your question," Robin said, smiling.

"Blackie can stay here if it's okay with your mom," Cole told Jeff. Then he turned to her. "Would that create a problem for you?"

Once more his gaze held hers, and once more she experienced that odd breathless sensation.

"I . . . No problem whatsoever."

Cole smiled then, and this time it was a smile so potent, so compelling, that it sailed straight through Robin's heart.

"MOM," JEFF HOLLERED as he burst through the front door late Thursday afternoon. "Kelly and Blackie and I are going to the fort."

"Kelly? Surely this isn't the *girl* named Kelly, is it? Not the one who lives next door?" Robin couldn't resist teasing her son. Apparently Jeff was willing to have a "pesky" girl for a friend, after all.

Jeff shrugged as he opened the cookie jar and groped inside. He frowned, not finding any cookies left and removed his hand, his fingertips covered with crumbs that he promptly licked off. "I found out Kelly isn't so bad."

"Have you got Blackie's leash?"

"We aren't going to need it. We're playing Sam Houston and Daniel Boone, and the Mexican army is

attacking. I'm going to smuggle Blackie out and go for
help. I can't use a leash for that."

"All right, just don't go any farther than the Alamo and be back by dinnertime."

"But that's less than an hour!" Jeff protested.

Robin gave him one of her don't-argue-with-me
looks.

"But I'm not hungry and—"

"Jeff," Robin said softly, widening her eyes just a
bit, increasing the intensity of her look.

"You know, Mom," Jeff said with a cry of undisguised disgust, "you don't fight fair." He hurried out
the front door with Blackie trotting faithfully behind.

Smiling to herself, Robin placed the meat loaf in the
oven and carried her coffee into the backyard. The
early evening air was filled with the scent of spring
flowers. A gentle breeze wafted over the budding trees.
How peaceful it seemed. How serene. All the years of
pinching pennies in order to save for a house of their
own seemed worth it now.

Her gaze wandered toward Cole Camden's yard.
Jeff, Kelly and Blackie were inside the fort, and she
could hear their raised voices every now and again.

Cole had been on her mind a great deal during the
past couple of days; she'd spent far too much time
dwelling on thoughts of her neighbor—about his rep-
utation in the neighborhood and the son he'd lost.

The tranquillity of the moment was shattered by the
insistent ringing of the phone. Robin walked briskly
to the kitchen, set her coffee on the counter and
reached for the receiver.

"Hello."

"Robin, it's Angela. I'm not catching you at a bad
time, am I?"

"No," Robin assured her. Angela worked in the same department as Robin, and over the years the two had become good friends. "What can I do for you?" she asked, as if she didn't already know.

"I'm calling to invite you to dinner—"

"On Saturday so I can meet your cousin Frank," Robin finished, rolling her eyes. Years before, Angela had taken on the task of finding Robin a husband. Never mind that Robin wasn't interested in meeting strangers! Angela couldn't seem to bear the thought of anyone spending her life alone and had appointed herself Robin's personal matchmaker.

"Frank's a really nice guy," Angela insisted. "I wouldn't steer you wrong, you know I wouldn't."

Robin restrained herself from reminding her friend of the disastrous date she'd arranged several weeks earlier.

"I've known Frank all my life," Angela said. "He's decent and nice."

"Decent" and "nice" were two words Robin had come to hate. Every man she'd ever met in this kind of arrangement was either decent or nice. Or both. Robin had come to think the two words were synonymous with dull, unattractive and emotionally manipulative. Generally these were recently divorced men who'd willingly placed themselves in the hands of family and friends to get them back into circulation.

"Didn't you tell me that Frank was recently divorced?" Robin asked.

"Yes, about six months ago now."

"Not interested."

"What do you mean you're not interested?" Angela demanded.

"I don't want to meet him. Angela, I know you mean well, and I apologize if I sound like a spoilsport, but I can't tell you the number of times I've had to nurse the fragile egos of recently divorced men. Most of the time they're emotional wrecks."

"But Frank's divorce was final months ago."

"If you still want me to meet him in a year, I'll be more than happy to have you arrange a dinner date."

Angela released a ragged sigh. "You're sure?"

"More than sure. Positive."

A short disappointed silence followed. "All right," Angela murmured in obvious frustration. "I'll see you in the morning."

"Right," Robin said, and because she felt guilty, she added, "I'll bring the coffee."

"Okay."

Robin lingered in the kitchen, frowning. She hated it when her friends put her on the spot this way. It was difficult enough to say no, but knowing that Angela's intentions were genuine made it even worse. Just as she was struggling with an attack of guilt, the phone rang again. Angela! Her friend must have suspected that Robin's offer to buy the coffee was a sign that she was weakening.

Gathering her fortitude, Robin seized the receiver and said firmly, "I'm not interested in dating Frank. I don't want to be rude, but that's final!"

Her abrupt words were followed by a short shocked silence, and then, "Robin, hello, this is Cole Camden."

"Cole," she gasped, closing her eyes. "Uh, I'm sorry, I thought you were someone else. A friend." She slumped against the wall and covered her face with one hand. "I have this friend who's keen on arranging dates for me, and she doesn't take no for an answer," Robin quickly explained. "I suppose you have friends wanting to arrange dates for you, too."

"Actually, I don't."

Of course he didn't. No doubt there were women all over San Francisco who longed to date Cole. He didn't require a personal matchmaker. All someone like him had to do was look interested and women would flock to his side.

Her hand tightened around the receiver and a sick weightless feeling attacked the pit of her stomach. "I apologize. I didn't mean to shout in your ear."

"You didn't."

"I suppose you called to talk to Jeff," she said. "He's with Blackie and Kelly—Kelly Lawrence, the little girl who lives on the other side of us."

"I see."

"He'll be back in a few minutes, if you'd like to call then. Or if you prefer, I could run and get him, but he said something about sneaking out and going for help and—"

"I beg your pardon? What's Jeff doing?"

"Oh, they're playing in the fort, pretending they're Houston and Daniel Boone. The fort is now the Alamo."

He chuckled. "I see. No, don't worry about chasing after him. I'd hate to see you waylaid by the Mexican army."

"I don't think I'd care for that myself."

"How's everything going?"

"Fine," she assured him.

She must have sounded rushed because he added, "You're sure this isn't a bad time? If you have company..."

"No, I'm here alone."

The short silence was broken by Cole. "So everything's going all right with Blackie? He isn't causing you any problems, is he?"

"Oh, no, everything's great. Jeff lavishes him with attention. The two of them are together practically every minute. Blackie even sleeps beside his bed."

"As you said, Jeff has a way with animals," Cole murmured.

His laugh, so tender and warm, was enough to jolt her equilibrium. She had to pinch herself to remember that Cole was a prominent attorney, wealthy and respected. She was an accountant. A junior accountant at that.

The only thing they had in common was the fact that they lived next door to each other and her son was crazy about his dog.

The silence returned, only this time it had a relaxed, almost comfortable quality, as though neither wanted the conversation to end.

"Since Jeff isn't around," Cole said reluctantly, "I'll let you go."

"I'll tell him you phoned."

"It wasn't anything important," Cole said. "Just wanted to let you know when I'll be back—late Friday afternoon. Will you be home?"

"Of course."

"You never know, your friend might talk you into going out with Fred after all."

"It's Frank, and there isn't a snowball's chance in hell."

"Famous last words!"

"See you Friday," she said with a short laugh.

"Right. Goodbye, Robin."

"Goodbye, Cole."

Long after the connection had been broken, Robin stood with her hand on the receiver, a smile touching her eyes and her heart.

"MOM, I NEED my lunch money," Jeff called impatiently from the bottom of the stairs.

"I'll be down in a minute," she answered. Mornings were crazy and always had been. In order to get to the Glen Park BART station on time, Robin had to leave the house a half hour before Jeff left for school.

"What did you have for breakfast?" she hollered down as she put the finishing touches on her makeup.

"Frozen waffles," Jeff shouted back. "And don't worry, I didn't drown them in syrup and I rinsed off the plate before I put it in the dishwasher."

"Rinsed it off or let Blackie lick it clean for you?" she asked, as she hurried down the stairs. Her son was busy at the sink and didn't turn around to look at her.

"Blackie, honestly, is that maple syrup on your nose?"

At the sound of his name, the Labrador trotted over to her. Robin took a moment to stroke his thick fur, before fumbling for her wallet to give Jeff his lunch money.

"Hey, Mom, you look nice."

"Don't sound so surprised," she grumbled. "I'm leaving now."

"Okay," Jeff said without the slightest bit of concern. "You won't be late tonight, will you? Remember Mr. Camden's due back."

"I remember, and no, I won't be late." She grabbed her packed lunch and headed for the front door.

Even before Robin arrived at the subway station, she knew the day would drag. Fridays always did.

She was right. At six, when the subway pulled into the station, Robin felt as though she'd been away forty hours instead of the usual nine. She found herself hurrying and didn't fully understand why. Cole was scheduled to return, but that didn't have anything to do with her, did it? His homecoming wasn't anything to feel nervous about, nor any reason to be pleased. He was her neighbor, and more Jeff's friend than hers.

The first thing Robin noticed when she arrived on Orchard Street was Cole's Porsche parked in the driveway of his house.

"Hi, Mom," Jeff called as he raced across the lawn between the two houses. "Mr. Camden's back."

"So I see." She removed her keys from her purse and opened the front door.

Jeff followed her inside. "He said he'd square up with me later. I wanted to invite him to dinner, but I didn't think I should without asking you first."

"That was smart," she said, depositing her jacket in the closet on her way into the kitchen. She opened the refrigerator and took out the thawed hamburger and salad makings.

"How was your day?" she asked.

Jeff sat down at the table and propped his elbows on it. "All right, I guess. What are you making for dinner?"

"Taco salad."

"How about just tacos? I don't understand why you want to ruin a perfectly good dinner by mixing green stuff with it."

Robin paused. "I thought you liked my taco salad."

Jeff shrugged. "It's all right, but I'd rather have just tacos." Once that was made clear, he cupped his chin in his hands. "Can we rent a video tonight?"

"I suppose," Robin returned absently as she added the meat to the onions browning in the skillet.

"But I get to choose this time," Jeff murmured. "Last week you picked out a musical." He wrinkled his nose as if to suggest being forced to watch men and women sing and dance was the most disgusting thing he'd ever had to endure.

"Perhaps we can find a compromise," she suggested.

Jeff nodded. "As long as it doesn't have a silly love story in it."

"Okay," Robin said, doing her best not to betray her amusement. Their difference in taste when it came to movies was legendary. Like most boys his age Jeff preferred gory thrillers, while Robin couldn't bear to rent anything violent. Unfortunately, her son was equally offended by the sight of men and women staring longingly into each other's eyes.

The meat was simmering in the skillet when Robin glanced up and noted that her son's look was surprisingly thoughtful. "Is something troubling you?" she asked, and popped a thin tomato slice into her mouth.

"Have you ever noticed that Mr. Camden never mentions he had a son?"

Robin set the paring knife against the cutting board. "It's probably painful for him to talk about."

Jeff nodded and with the innocent wisdom of youth, he whispered, "That man needs someone."

THE MEAL WAS FINISHED, and Robin was standing in front of the sink rinsing off the dinner plates when the doorbell rang. Robin knew it had to be Cole.

"I'll get it," Jeff cried as he raced past her at breakneck speed. He threw open the door with enough enthusiasm to tear it from its hinges. "Hi, Mr. Camden!" he said eagerly.

By this time Robin had smoothed her peach-colored sweater over her slim hips and placed a friendly—but not too friendly—smile on her face. At the last second, she ran her fingers through her hair, striving for the casual I-didn't-go-to-any-trouble look, then wondered at her irrational behavior. Cole wasn't coming over to see *her.*

Robin could hear Jeff chatting away at ninety miles an hour, telling Cole they were renting a movie and how Robin insisted that every show he saw had to have the proper rating, which he claimed was totally ridiculous. He went on to explain that she considered choosing the film a mother's job and apparently a mere kid didn't have rights. When there was a pause in the conversation, she could envision Jeff rolling his eyes dramatically.

Taking a deep breath, she stepped into the entryway and smiled. "Hello, Cole."

"Robin."

Their eyes met instantly. Dark brown sought out light blue. Robin's first coherent thought was that a woman could get lost in eyes that dark and not even care. She swallowed tightly and lowered her gaze.

"Would you care for a cup of coffee?" she asked, having difficulty dragging the words out of her mouth.

"If it isn't too much trouble."

"It isn't." At least it wouldn't be if she could stop her heart from pounding so furiously.

"Where's Blackie?" Jeff demanded, opening the screen door and glancing outside.

"I didn't bring him over. I thought you'd be thoroughly tired of him by now."

"Tired of Blackie?" Jeff cried. "You've got to be kidding!"

"I take it I should have known better," Cole teased.

Robin returned to the kitchen and took mugs from the cupboard, using these few moments to compose herself.

The screen door slammed, and a moment later Cole appeared in her kitchen. "Jeff went over to my house to get Blackie."

She smiled and nodded. "Do you take cream or sugar?" she asked, tossing the question over her shoulder.

"Just black, thanks."

Robin normally drank hers the same way. But for some reason she couldn't begin to fathom, she added a generous teaspoonful of sugar to her own, stirring briskly as though she feared it wouldn't dissolve.

"I hope your trip went well," she said, carrying both mugs into the family room where Cole had chosen to sit.

"Very well."

"Good." She sat a safe distance from him, across the room in a wooden rocker, and balanced her mug on her knee. "Everything went without a hitch around here, but I fear Jeff may have spoiled Blackie a bit."

"From what he said, they did everything but attend school together."

"Having the dog around has been wonderful for him. I appreciate your giving Jeff this opportunity. Not only does it satisfy his need for a dog, but it's taught him about responsibility."

The front door opened and the canine subject of their conversation shot into the room, followed by Jeff, who was grinning from ear to ear. "Mom, would it be all right if Mr. Camden stayed and watched the movie with us?"

"Ah..." Caught off guard, Robin didn't know what to say. After being away from home several days, watching a move with his neighbors probably held a low position on Cole's list of priorities.

To Robin's surprise, Cole's eyes searched hers as though seeking her approval.

"You'd be welcome...I mean, you can stay if you'd like, unless there's something else you'd rather do. I mean, I'd ...we'd like it if you did, but..." She let whatever else she might have said fade away. She was making a mess of this, and every time she tried to smooth it over, she only stuck her foot further down her throat.

"What movie have you rented?"

"We haven't yet," Jeff explained. "Mom and me had to come to an understanding first. She likes the mushy stuff and gets all bent out of shape if there's a little blood. You wouldn't believe the love story she forced me to watch last Friday night." His voice dipped with renewed disgust.

"How about if you and I go rent the movie while your mother and Blackie make the popcorn?"

Jeff's blue eyes brightened immediately. "That'd be great, wouldn't it, Mom?"

"Sure," she agreed, and was rewarded by Jeff's eager smile.

Jeff and Cole left a few minutes later. It was on the tip of her tongue to give Cole instructions on the type of movie appropriate for a ten-year-old boy, but she swallowed her concerns, willing to trust his judgment. Standing on the porch, she watched as the two climbed inside Cole's expensive sports car. She pressed her hand to her throat, grateful when Cole leaned over the front seat and snapped Jeff's seat belt snugly in place. Her son must have commented on how Robin made him wear a seat belt, too, because Cole's gaze flew to her. She raised her hand in farewell, and Cole did the same. It was a simple gesture, yet Robin felt as if they'd communicated so much more than a simple farewell.

"Come on, Blackie," Robin said, "let's go start the popcorn." The devoted Lab trailed behind her as she returned to the kitchen. She set the old battered pot on the stove and turned on the burner, heating a generous amount of vegetable oil, then adding kernels. It was while she was waiting for the first few to pop that the words slipped from her mouth.

"Well, Lonny, what do you think?" Talking to her dead husband came without conscious thought. It certainly wasn't that she expected him to answer. Whenever she spoke to him, the words came spontaneously from the deep well of love they'd once shared. She supposed she should feel foolish doing it, but so many times over the long years since he'd died, she had felt his presence and his love. Robin assumed that the reason she talked to him was born out of a need to discuss things with the one other person who'd loved her son as much as she did. In the beginning she was sure she needed to visit a psychiatrist or arrange for grief counseling, but later she convinced herself that every widow went through this in one form or another.

"He's grown so much the past year, hasn't he?" she asked, and smiled. "Meeting Cole has been good for Jeff. He lost a child, you know, and I suppose having Jeff move in next door answers a need for him, too."

The first kernels of corn popped and Robin transferred her attention to the pot, gripping its faded black handle and shaking it gently.

A couple of minutes later, Jeff and Cole returned with a movie that turned out to be an excellent compromise—a teenage comedy that was surprisingly witty and entertaining.

Jeff sprawled on the carpet munching popcorn with Blackie by his side. Cole sat on the sofa and Robin chose the rocking chair. She removed her shoes and tucked her feet beneath her. She was enjoying the movie; in fact, several times she found herself laughing outright.

Cole and Jeff laughed, too. The sounds were contrasting—one deep and masculine, the other young and pleasantly boyish—yet they harmonized, blending with perfect naturalness.

Soon Robin found herself watching Jeff and Cole more than the movie. The two...no, the three of them were comfortable together. Robin didn't try to read any significance into that. Doing so could prove emotionally dangerous, but the thought flew into her mind and refused to leave.

The credits were rolling when Cole pointed to Jeff, whose head was resting on his arms. For the first time, Robin noted that her son's eyes were closed.

"He's asleep," Cole said softly.

Robin smiled and nodded. She got up to carry the empty popcorn bowls into the kitchen. Cole stood, too, taking their glasses to the sink, then returned to the family room to rewind the movie.

"Do you want me to carry him upstairs for you?" he asked, glancing down on the slumbering Jeff.

"No," she whispered. "When he wakes up in the morning, he'll think you treated him like a little kid. Egos are surprisingly fragile at ten."

"I suppose you're right."

The silence felt as loud as thunder to Robin. Without Jeff, awake and chattering, as a buffer between them, she felt clumsy and self-conscious around Cole.

"It was nice of you to stay," she said, more to fill the quiet than because she had anything important to communicate. "It meant a lot to Jeff."

Jeff had mentioned that Cole had an active social life. Heather Lawrence had confirmed it by casually letting it drop that Cole was often away on weekends. Robin wasn't entirely sure what to think about it all. If there was a woman in his life, that was his business, not hers.

"It meant a lot to me, too," he said, standing in front of the VCR while he waited for the movie to finish rewinding.

The kitchen and family room, actually quite spacious, felt close and intimate with Cole standing only a few feet away.

Robin's fingers were shaking as she stacked the bowls and soda glasses in the dishwasher. She tried to think of some bright and witty comment to make, but her mind was blank.

"I should be going."

Was that reluctance she heard in his voice? Somehow Robin doubted it; probably wishful thinking on her part. Half of her wanted to push him out the door and the other half didn't want him to leave so early. But there really wasn't any reason for him to stay. "I'll walk you to the door."

"Blackie." Cole called for his dog. "It's time to go."

The Lab didn't look pleased with this turn of events. He took his own sweet time lumbering to his feet and stretching his long sleek body before trotting to Cole's side.

Robin was about to open the door when she realized she hadn't thanked Cole for getting the movie. She turned, and his dark eyes delved into hers. Whatever thoughts had been taking shape in her mind fled like leaves scattering in the wind. She tried to smile, however weakly, but it was difficult when he was looking at her so intently. His gaze slipped to her mouth, and in a nervous movement, she moistened her lips. Before she was fully aware of how it had happened, Cole's fingers were in her hair and he was lifting her mouth to meet his.

His eyes held hers, as if he expected her to stop him, then they slowly closed and his mouth grazed hers. Robin's eyes drifted shut, but that was the only response she made.

He kissed her again, even more gently than the first time. His lips were tender, and Robin moaned softly, not in protest, but in wonder and surprise. It had been so long since a man had kissed her like this. So long that Robin had forgotten the wealth of sensations a mere kiss could evoke. Her hands crept to his chest, and her fingers curled into the soft wool of his sweater.

Hesitantly, timidly, her lips trembled beneath his, parting as the kiss blossomed. Cole sighed and took full possession of her mouth.

Robin sighed, too. The tears that welled in her eyes were a shock. She was at a loss to explain where they came from or why. They silently slipped down her face, and it wasn't until she felt the moisture that she realized she was crying.

Cole must have felt the tears at the same moment as she had, because he abruptly broke off the kiss and raised his head. His eyes searched hers as his thumb brushed the moisture from her cheek.

"Did I hurt you?" The question was whispered.

She shook her head vehemently.

"Then why...?"

"I don't know." She couldn't explain something she didn't understand herself. Rubbing the heels of her hands across her eyes, she attempted to wipe away the evidence. She forced a smile and looked up at him. "I'm nothing if not novel," she said with brittle cheerfulness. "I don't imagine many women break into tears when you kiss them."

Cole looked as confused as Robin felt.

"Don't worry about it. I'm fine." She wanted to reassure him, but was having too much trouble analyzing her own reactions to answer his doubts.

"Let's sit down and talk about this."

"No," she said quietly. Adamantly. That was the last thing she wanted. "I'm sorry, Cole. I really am. This has never happened before and I'm at as much of a loss to understand it as you are."

"But..."

"The best thing we can do is chalk it up to a long tiring work week."

"It's not that simple."

"Probably, but I'd prefer to just forget it. Please?"

"Are you all right?"

"Emotionally or physically?" She tried to joke, but didn't succeed.

"Both."

He was so serious, so concerned, that it was all Robin could do not to dissolve into a fit of fresh tears. She'd made a world-class fool of herself with this man, not once but twice.

This man, who had suffered such a tremendous loss himself, was so gentle, so tender with her, and instead of helping, it only made matters worse. "I'm sorry, really I am," she said raggedly, "but I think you should go home now."

CHAPTER FOUR

"YOU KNOW WHAT I'm in the mood for?" Angela Lansky said as she sat on the edge of Robin's desk early Monday afternoon.

"I certainly hope you're going to say food," Robin teased. The two shared the same lunch hour and were celebrating a cost-of-living raise by eating out.

"A shrimp salad," Angela elaborated. "Heaped six inches high with big fresh shrimp."

"I was thinking Chinese food myself," Robin said, "but now that you mention it, shrimp salad sounds good." She opened her bottom drawer and withdrew her purse.

Angela was short and enviably thin with thick brown hair that fell in natural waves over her slim shoulders. She used clips to hold the abundant curls away from her face and looked closer to twenty than the thirty-five Robin knew her to be.

"I know just the place," Angela insisted. "The Blue Crab. It's on the wharf and worth the trouble of getting there."

"I'm game," Robin said.

They stopped at the bank to deposit their checks, and then headed for the restaurant. They decided to catch the Market Street cable car to Fisherman's Wharf. After purchasing their tokens they joined the quickly growing line.

"So how's the kid doing?" Angela asked. She and her salesman husband didn't plan to have children themselves, but Angela enjoyed hearing about Jeff.

"He signed up for baseball through the park program and starts practice this week. I think it'll be good for him. He was terribly lonely this weekend now that Blackie's back with Cole."

"But isn't Blackie over at your place as much as he was before?" Angela asked.

Robin shook her head. "Cole left early Saturday morning and apparently took his dog with him. Jeff moped around for most of the weekend like a lost puppy, so to speak."

"Where'd your handsome neighbor go?"

"Good grief, how am I supposed to know that?" Robin countered with a soft laugh, hiding her disappointment at his disappearance. "Cole doesn't clear his schedule with me."

The way he'd left—without a word of farewell or explanation—still hurt. It was the kind of hurt that came from realizing what a complete fool she'd made of herself with this worldly, sophisticated man. He'd kissed her and she'd started weeping. Good lord, he was probably doing back flips in order to avoid seeing her again, and she couldn't blame him.

"Do you think Cole was with a woman?"

"That's none of my business!"

"But I thought your neighbor said Cole spent his weekends with a woman friend."

Robin didn't remember mentioning that to Angela, but she obviously had, along with practically everything else. Robin had tried to convince herself that confiding in Angela about Cole was a clever way of thwarting her friend's matchmaking efforts. Unfortunately, the whole thing had backfired in her face. In the end the last person she wanted to talk about was Cole, but of course Angela persisted in questioning her.

"Well?" Angela demanded. "Did he spend his weekend with a woman or not?"

"What he does with his time is his business, not mine," Robin reiterated. She pretended not to care. But she did. Too damn much. She'd promised herself she wasn't going to put any stock in the kiss or the powerful attraction she felt for Cole. Within the space of one evening, she'd wiped out every pledge she'd made to herself. She hadn't said anything to Jeff—how could she?—but she was just as disappointed as he was that Cole had left for the weekend.

"I was hoping something might develop between the two of you," Angela murmured. "Since you're obviously not interested in meeting Frank, it would be great if you got something going with your neighbor."

Robin cast her a plaintive look that suggested otherwise. "Cole Camden lives in the fanciest house in the neighborhood. He's a partner in the law firm of Blackwell, Burns and Dailey, which we both know is one of the most prestigious in San Francisco. And he drives a car with a name I can barely pronounce. Now what would someone like that see in me?"

"Lots of things," Angela countered.

Robin snickered. "I hate to disillusion you, my friend, but the only thing Cole Camden and I have in common is the fact that my small yard borders his massive one."

"Maybe," Angela agreed, raising her eyebrows. "But I noticed something different about you from the first time you mentioned him."

"That's ridiculous."

"It isn't," Angela insisted. "I've watched you with other men over the past few years. A guy will show some interest, and at first everything looks peachy-keen. You'll go out with him a couple of times, maybe even more, but before anything serious can develop, you've broken off the relationship without ever really giving it a chance."

Robin didn't have much of an argument, since that was true, but she made a token protest just the same. "I can't help it if I have high standards."

"High standards!" Angela choked back a laugh. "That's got to be the understatement of the century. You'd find fault with Prince Charming."

Robin rolled her eyes, but couldn't hold back a smile. Angela was right, although that certainly hadn't slowed her matchmaking efforts.

"From the time you first mentioned your neighbor," Angela went on, "I noticed something different about you, and frankly, I'm thrilled. In all the years we've known each other, this is the first time I can remember you giving a man this much attention. Until now, it's always been the other way around."

"I'm not interested in Cole," she mumbled. "Oh, honestly, Angela, I can't imagine where you come up with these ideas. I think you've been reading too many romance novels."

Angela waved her index finger under Robin's nose. "Listen, my friend, I'm on to you. You're not going to divert me with humor, or weasel your way out of admitting it. You can't fool me—you're attracted to this guy and it's frightening you to death. Right?''

The two women gazed solemnly at each other, both too stubborn to admit defeat. Under the force of her friend's unyielding determination, Robin was the one who finally gave in.

''All right!'' she cried, causing the other people waiting for the cable car to turn and stare. ''All right,'' she repeated in a whisper. ''I like Cole, but for the life of me I don't understand it.''

Angela's winged brows arched speculatively. ''He's attractive and wealthy, crazy about your son, generous and kind, and you haven't figured it out yet?''

''He's also way out of my league.''

''I wish you'd quit categorizing yourself. You make it sound as though you aren't good enough for him, and that's ridiculous.''

Robin just sighed.

The cable car appeared then, its bell clanging as it drew to a stop. Robin and Angela boarded and held on tightly.

Jeff loved hearing about the history of the cable cars, and Robin loved telling him the story. Andrew Hallidie had designed them because of his deep love for horses. Day after day, Hallidie had watched them struggling up and down the treacherous hills of the city, carting heavy burdens. Prompted by his concern for the animals, he'd invented the cable cars that are pulled by a continuously moving underground cable. To Jeff and to many others, Andrew Hallidie was a hero.

Robin and Angela were immediately caught up by the festive atmosphere of Fisherman's Wharf. The rows of fishing boats along the dock bobbed gently with the tide, and although Robin had never been to the Mediterranean, the view reminded her of pictures she'd seen of French and Italian harbors.

The day was beautiful, the sky blue and cloudless, the ocean sparkling the way it did on a summer day. The entire spring had been exceptionally warm. It wasn't uncommon for Robin to wear a winter coat in the middle of July, especially in the mornings when there was often a heavy fog accompanied by a cool mist from the Bay. But this spring, they'd experienced some lovely weather, including today's.

"Let's eat alfresco," Angela suggested, spying a free table outside the restaurant.

"All right," Robin agreed cheerfully. The Blue Crab was a popular restaurant and one of several in a long row that lined the wharf. More elegant dining took place inside, but the sidewalk was crowded with diners interested in a less formal meal.

Once they were seated, Robin and Angela were waited on quickly, and they promptly ordered their shrimp salads.

"So," Angela murmured, spreading her napkin over her lap while closely studying Robin. "Tell me more about your neighbor."

Robin froze. "I thought we were finished with this subject. In case you hadn't noticed, I'd prefer not to discuss Cole."

"I noticed, but unfortunately I was just getting started. It's a novelty for you to be so keen on a man, and I know hardly anything about him. It's time, Robin Masterson, to tell all."

"There's nothing to talk about. I already told you everything I care to," Robin answered crossly. She briefly wondered if Angela had guessed that Cole had kissed her. At the rate things were going, she was probably going to drag it out of her before lunch was over. Robin sincerely wished she could think of some clever way to change the subject.

Tall glasses of iced tea arrived and Robin was reaching for a packet of sugar when she heard a masculine chuckle that reminded her instantly of Cole. She paused, savoring the husky sound. Without really meaning to, she found herself scanning the tables, certain Cole was seated only a short distance away.

"He's here," she whispered before she could guard her tongue.

"Who?"

"Cole. I just heard him laugh."

Pushing back her chair in order to get a fuller view of the inside dining area, Robin searched through a sea of faces, but didn't find her neighbor's.

"What's he look like?" Angela whispered.

Ten different ways to describe him shot through her mind. To say he had brown hair, neatly trimmed, coffee-colored eyes and was about six foot two seemed inadequate. To add that he was strikingly attractive in ways she didn't know how to explain further complicated the problem.

"Tell me what to look for," Angela insisted. "Come on, Robin, this is a golden opportunity. I want to get a good look at this guy. I'm not about to let a chance like this slip through my fingers. I bet he's gorgeous."

Reluctantly, Robin continued to scan the diners, but she didn't see anyone who remotely resembled Cole. Even if she did see him, she wasn't completely sure she'd point him out to Angela, although she hated to lie. Perhaps she wouldn't have to. Perhaps she'd imagined the whole thing. It would have been easy enough to do. Angela's questions had brought Cole to the forefront of her mind; they'd just been discussing him and it was only natural for her to—

Her heart pounded against her rib cage with the force of a wrecking ball as Cole walked out of the restaurant foyer. He wasn't alone. A tall, slender woman with legs that seemed to go all the way to her neck and a figure as shapely and athletic as a dancer's was standing at his side. She was blond and, in a word, gorgeous. Robin felt as appealing as milk weed in comparison. The woman's arm was delicately tucked in Cole's, and she was smiling up at him with eyes big and blue enough to turn heads.

Robin's stomach tightened into a hard knot.

"Robin," Angela said anxiously, leaning toward her, "what is it?"

Cole was strolling past them, and in an effort not to be seen, Robin quickly stuck her head under the table pretending to search for her purse.

"Robin," Angela muttered, lowering her own head and peeking under the linen tablecloth, "what's the matter with you?"

"Nothing." Other than the fact that she was going to be ill. Other than the fact that she'd never been more outclassed in her life. "I'm fine, really." A smile trembled on her pale lips.

"Then what are you doing with your head under the table?"

"I don't suppose you'd believe my napkin fell off my lap?"

"No."

A pair of shiny black shoes appeared. Slowly, reluctantly, Robin twisted her head and glanced upward, squinting at the flash of sunlight that nearly

blinded her. It was their waiter. Heaving a giant sigh
of relief, Robin straightened. The first thing she noticed was that Cole had left.

The huge shrimp salads were all but forgotten as
Angela, eyes narrowed and elbows braced on the table, confronted her. "You saw him, didn't you?"

It wouldn't do any good to pretend otherwise, so
Robin nodded.

"I take it he was with someone?"

"Not just someone! Miss Universe was draped all
over his arm."

"That doesn't mean anything," Angela said.
"Don't you think you're jumping to conclusions?
Honestly, she could have been anyone."

"Right." Any fight left in Robin had long since
evaporated. There was nothing like seeing Cole with
another woman to bring her firmly back to earth—
which was right where she belonged.

She could have been a client.

"She probably was," Robin concurred, reaching for
her fork. She didn't know how she was going to manage one shrimp, let alone a whole plate of them.
Heaving another huge sigh, she plowed her fork into
the heap of plump pink darlings. It was then that she
happened to glance across the street. Cole and Miss
Universe were walking along the sidewalk, gazing intently at each other. For some reason, known only to
the fates, Cole looked across the street at that very
moment. His gaze instantly narrowed in on her. He
stopped midstride as though shocked to have seen her.

Doing her best to pretend she hadn't seen *him,*
Robin took another bite of her salad and chewed
vigorously. When she glanced up again, Cole was
gone.

"Mom, I need someone to practice with," Jeff pleaded. He stood forlornly in front of her, a baseball mitt in one hand, a ball in the other.

"I thought Jimmy was practicing with you."

"He had to go home and then Kelly tossed me a few pitches, but she had to go home, too. Besides, she's a girl."

"What am I?" Robin muttered. "Chopped liver?"

"You're a mom," Jeff answered, clearly not understanding her question. "Don't you see? I've got a chance of making pitcher for our team if I can get someone to practice with me."

"All right," Robin agreed, grumbling a bit. She set aside her needlepoint and followed her son into the backyard. He handed her his old catcher's mitt, which barely fit her hand, and positioned her with her back to Cole's yard.

Robin hadn't been able to completely avoid her neighbor in the past week, but she'd managed to keep her distance. For that matter, he didn't seem all that eager to run into her, either. Just as well, she supposed.

He stayed on his side of the hedge. She stayed on hers.

If he passed her on his way to work, he gave an absent wave. She returned the gesture.

If they happened to be outside at the same time, they exchanged smiles and a polite greeting, but nothing more. It seemed, although Robin couldn't be sure, that Cole spent less time outside than usual. For that matter so did she.

"Okay," Jeff called, running to the end of their yard. "Squat down."

"I beg your pardon?" Robin shouted indignantly. "I agreed to play catch with you. You didn't say anything about having to squat!"

"Mom," Jeff said impatiently, "think about it. If I'm going to be the pitcher, you've got to be the catcher, and all catchers have to be low to the ground."

Muttering complaints under her breath, Robin sank to her knees, worried the grass would stain her jeans.

Jeff tossed his arms into the air in abject frustration. "Not like that!" He said something more that Robin couldn't quite make out—something about why couldn't moms be guys.

Reluctantly, Robin assumed the posture he wanted, but she didn't know how long her knees would hold out. Jeff wound up his arm and let loose with a fastball. Robin closed her eyes, stuck out the mitt and was so shocked when she caught the ball that she toppled backward into the wet grass.

"You all right?" Jeff yelled, racing toward her.

"I'm fine, I'm fine," she shouted back, discounting his concern as she brushed the dampness from the seat of her pants. She righted herself, assumed the position and waited for the second ball.

Jeff raced back to his mock pitcher's mound, gripped both hands behind his back and stepped forward. Robin closed her eyes again. Nothing happened. She opened her eyes cautiously, puzzled about the delay. Then she recalled the hand movements she'd seen pitchers make in the movies and flexed her fingers a few times.

Jeff straightened, placed his hand on his hip and stared at her. "What was that for?"

"It's a signal . . . I think. I saw the guy in the movie *Bull Durham* do it."

"Mom, leave that kind of stuff to the guys in the movies. All I want you to do is catch my pitches and throw them back. It might help if you kept your eyes open, too."

"I'll try."

"Thank you, I appreciate that."

Robin suspected she heard a tinge of sarcasm in her son's voice. She didn't know what he was getting so riled up about; she was doing her best. It was times such as these that she most longed for Lonny. When her parents had still lived in the area, Jeff's grandfather had stepped in whenever her son needed a father's guiding hand, but they'd moved to Arizona a couple of years ago. Lonny's family had been in Texas since just before his death. Robin hadn't seen them since the funeral, although Lonny's mother faithfully sent Jeff birthday and Christmas gifts.

"You ready?" Jeff shouted.

"Ready." Squinting, Robin stuck out the mitt, prepared to do her best to catch the silly ball, since it seemed so important to her son. Once more he swung his arms behind him and stepped forward. Then he stood there, poised to throw, for what seemed an eternity. Her knees were beginning to ache.

"Are you going to throw the ball, or are you going to stare at me all night?" she asked after a long moment had passed.

"That does it," Jeff shouted, tossing his mitt to the ground. "You just broke my concentration."

"Well, for crying out loud, what's there to concentrate about?" Robin muttered, rising awkwardly to her feet. Her legs had started to lose feeling, the way she'd crouched there, balanced on her toes.

"This isn't working," Jeff cried, stalking toward her. "Kelly's only in third grade and she does a better job than you do."

Robin decided to let that comment pass. She pressed her hand to the small of her back, hoping to ease the ache she was beginning to feel.

"Hello, Robin. Jeff."

Cole's voice came at her like a hangman's noose. She straightened abruptly and winced at the sharp pain that shot through her back.

"Hi, Mr. Camden!" Jeff shouted as though Cole was a conquering hero returned from the war. He raced across the yard, past Robin and straight to the hedge. "Where have you been all week? I've hardly seen you."

"I've been busy." He might have been talking to Jeff, but his eyes were holding Robin's. She tried to look away—but she couldn't.

His eyes told her she was avoiding him.

Hers answered that he'd been avoiding her.

His said it was time for things to change.

Her eyes suggested she'd rather things continue as they were.

"I guess you *have* been busy," Jeff was saying. "I haven't seen you in days and days and days." Blackie squeezed through the hedge and Jeff fell to his knees, his arms circling the dog's neck lovingly.

"So how's the baseball going?" Cole asked.

Jeff sent his mother a disgusted look, then shrugged. "All right, I guess."

"What position are you playing?"

"Probably outfield. I had a chance to make pitcher, but I can't seem to get anyone who knows how to catch a baseball to work with me. Kelly tries, but she's a girl and I hate to say it, but my own mother is worthless."

"I did my best," Robin felt obliged to remind him.

"She catches with her eyes closed," Jeff said.

"How about if you toss a few balls at me?" Cole offered.

Jeff blinked as if he thought he'd misunderstood their neighbor. "You want me to throw you a few pitches? You're sure?"

"Positive."

The look on her son's face defied description as Cole hopped over the hedge. Jeff's smile stretched from one side of his face to the other as he tore to the opposite side of the yard, unwilling to question Cole's generosity a second time.

For an awkward moment, Robin stayed where she was, not knowing what to say. Her heart was full of gratitude, as full as Jeff's smile. She looked up at Cole, her emotions soaring—and tangling like kite strings in a brisk wind. She was deeply grateful for his offer, but also confused. Thrilled by his presence, but also frightened.

"Mom?" Jeff muttered. "In case you hadn't noticed, you're in the way."

"Are you going to make coffee and invite me in for a chat later?" Cole asked quietly.

Her heart sank to the pit of her stomach. "I have some things that need to be done, and . . . and . . ."

"Mom?" Jeff shouted a second time.

"I think it's time you and I talked," Cole said, staring straight into her eyes.

"Mom, are you moving or not?"

She tossed a frantic look over her shoulder. "Oh...oh, sorry," she whispered, blushing. Robin hurried away, then stood on the patio watching as the ball flew across the yard a couple of times with a speed that amazed her.

After catching a dozen of Jeff's pitches, Cole got up and walked over to her son. They spoke for several minutes. Reluctantly, Robin decided it was time to go back in.

It astonished her how hard and loud her heart was pounding. She busied herself wiping counters that were already perfectly clean and tried to stop thinking about the beautiful woman she'd seen with Cole on the Wharf.

Jeff stormed into the house fifteen minutes later. "Mom, would it be all right if Mr. Camden strings up an old tire from the apple tree?"

"I suppose. Why?"

"He said I can use it to practice pitching, and I wouldn't need to trouble you or Kelly."

"I don't think I have an old tire."

"Don't worry, Mr. Camden has one." He ran outside again before she could comment.

Jeff was back in the yard with Cole a few minutes later, far too soon to suit Robin. She forced a weak smile to her lips. That other woman was a perfect damsel to his knight in shining armor, she thought wryly. Robin, on the other hand, considered herself more of a court jester.

Her musings were abruptly halted when Cole walked into the kitchen, trailed by her son.

"Isn't it time for you to take your bath, Jeff?" Cole asked pointedly.

It looked for a minute as though the boy was going to argue. For the first time in recent memory, Robin would have welcomed some resistance from him.

"I guess," he said. Bathing was about as popular as homework.

"I didn't make any coffee," Robin said in a small voice. She simply couldn't look at Cole and not see the beautiful blonde on his arm.

"That's fine. I'm more interested in talking than drinking coffee, anyway," he said. He walked purposefully to the table and pulled out a chair. He gestured for her to sit down.

Robin didn't. Instead, she examined her watch. "My goodness, will you look at the time?"

"No." Cole headed toward her, and Robin backed slowly into the counter.

He should never have kissed her. She should never have allowed it.

"We're going talk about that kiss," Cole warned her.

"Please, don't," she whispered. "It meant nothing! We'd both had a hectic week. We were tired.... I wasn't myself."

Cole's eyes burned into hers. "Then why did you cry?"

"I . . . don't know. Believe me if I knew I'd tell you, but I don't. Can't we just forget it ever happened?"

His shoulders heaved once in a silent sigh as he threaded his long fingers through his hair. "That's exactly what I've tried to do all week. Unfortunately it didn't work."

CHAPTER FIVE

"I'VE PUT IT COMPLETELY out of my mind," Robin said, continuing her string of untruths. "I wish you'd do the same."

"I can't. Trust me, I've tried," Cole told her softly. He smiled and his sensuous mouth widened as his eyes continued to hold hers. The messages were back. Less than subtle messages. *You can't fool me,* they said, and *I didn't want to admit it either.*

"I . . ."

The sense of expectancy was written in clean, clear strokes across his face. For the life of her, Robin couldn't tear her eyes from him.

She didn't remember stepping into his arms, but suddenly she was there, encompassed by his warmth, feeling more sheltered and protected than she had since her husband's death. This comforting sensation spun itself around her as he wove his fingers into her hair, cradling her head. He hadn't kissed her yet, but Robin felt the promise of it in every part of her.

Deny it though she might, she knew in her heart how badly she wanted Cole to hold her, to kiss her. He must have read the longing in her eyes, because he lowered his mouth to hers, stopping a fraction of an inch from her parted lips. She could feel warm moist breath, could feel a desire so powerful, she wanted to drown in his kiss.

From a reservoir of strength she didn't know she possessed, Robin managed to shake her head. "No...please."

"Yes...please," he whispered just before his mouth settled firmly over hers.

His kiss was the same as it had been before, only more intense. More potent. Robin felt rocked to the very core of her being. Against every dictate of her will, she felt herself surrendering to him. She felt herself forgetting to breathe. She felt herself weakening.

His mouth moved to the delicate line of her jaw, spreading small, soft kisses there. She sighed. She couldn't help it. Cole's touch was magic, and the walls guarding her heart were threatened for the first time in almost ten years. Unable to stop herself, she turned her head to the other side, yearning for him to trace a row of kisses there, as well. He complied.

Once more, Robin sighed, her mind filled with traitorous, sensuous thoughts. It felt so good in his arms, so warm and safe...but she knew the feeling was deceptive. She'd seen him with another woman, one far better suited to him than she could ever be. For days she'd been tormented by the realization that the woman in the restaurant was probably the one he spent his weekends with.

"No, please don't." Once more she pleaded, but even to her own ears, the words held little conviction.

In response, Cole delivered a long slow series of feather-light kisses to her lips, effectively silencing any protest. Robin trembled, breathless.

"Why are you fighting me so hard?" Cole whispered. His hands framed her face, his thumbs stroking her cheeks. They were damp and she hadn't even realized she was crying.

She heard the sudden sound of footsteps bounding down the stairs. At the thought of Jeff finding her in Cole's arms, she abruptly broke away and turned to stare out the darkened window, hoping for a moment to compose herself.

Jeff burst into the room. "Did you kiss her yet?" he demanded of Cole. Not waiting for an answer, Jeff raced toward Robin and grabbed her by the hand. "Well, Mom, what do you think?"

"About what?"

"Mr. Camden kissing you. He did, didn't he?"

It was on the tip of her tongue to deny the whole thing, but she decided to brazen it out. "You want me to rate him? Like on a scale of one to ten?"

Jeff blinked, uncertain. His questioning glance flew to Cole.

"She was a ten," Cole said out of the corner of his mouth.

"A . . . high seven," Robin returned.

"A high seven!" Jeff cried, casting her a disparaging look. He shook his head and walked over to Cole. "She's out of practice," he said confidingly. "Doesn't know how to rate guys. Give her a little time and she'll come around."

"Jeff," Robin gasped, thoroughly amazed to be having this type of discussion with her son, let alone Cole, who was looking all too smug.

"She hardly goes out at all," Jeff added. "My mom's got this friend who arranges dates for her, and you wouldn't believe some of the guys she's been stuck with. One of them came to the door—"

"Jeff," Robin said sharply, "that's enough!"

"But one of us needs to explain."

"Mr. Camden was just leaving," Robin said, glaring at her neighbor, daring him to contradict her.

"I was? Oh, yeah. Your mom was just about to walk me to the door, isn't that right, Robin?"

She gaped at Cole as he reached for her hand and gently led her in the direction of the front door. Meekly she submitted, but not before she saw Jeff give Cole a thumbs-up.

"All right," Cole said, standing in the entryway, his hands heavy on her shoulders. "I want to know what's wrong."

"Wrong? Nothing's wrong."

"It's because of Victoria, isn't it?"

"Victoria?" she asked, already knowing that had to be the woman with him the day she'd seen him at the Blue Crab.

"Yes. Victoria. I saw you practically hiding under your table, pretending you didn't notice me."

"I . . . Why should I care?" She hated the way her voice shook.

"Yes, why should you?"

She didn't answer him. Couldn't answer him. She told herself it didn't matter that he was with another woman. Then again, it mattered more than she dared admit.

"Tell me," he insisted.

Robin lowered her gaze. If only he'd stop holding her, stop touching her. Then she might be able to think clearly. "You looked right together. She was a perfect complement to you. She's tall and blond and—"

"Cold as an iceberg. Victoria's a business associate—we had lunch together. Nothing more. I find her as appealing as . . . as dirty laundry."

"Please, don't explain. It's none of my business who you have lunch with or who you date or where you go every weekend or who you're with. Really. I shouldn't have said anything. I don't know why I did. It was wrong of me—very wrong. I can't believe we're even talking about this."

Jeff's head shot out from the kitchen. "How are things going in here?"

"Good," Robin said. "I was just telling Cole how much we both appreciated his help with your pitching."

"I was having real problems until Cole came along," Jeff confirmed. "Girls are good for some things, but serious baseball isn't one of them."

Robin opened the front door. "Thanks," she whispered, her eyes avoiding Cole's, "for everything."

"Everything?"

She blushed, remembering the kisses they'd shared. But before she could think of a witty reply, Cole brushed his lips across hers.

"Hey, Cole," Jeff cried, running to the front door. "I've got a baseball game Thursday night. Can you come?"

"I'd love to," Cole answered, his eyes holding Robin's. Then he turned abruptly and strode out the door.

"JEFF, WE'RE GOING TO BE LATE for the game if we don't leave now."

"But Cole isn't home yet," Jeff protested. "He said he'd be here."

"There's probably a very good explanation," Robin stated calmly, although she was as disappointed as Jeff. "He could be tied up in traffic, or delayed at the office, or any one of a thousand other things. He wouldn't purposely not come.''

"Do you think he forgot?''

"I'm sure he didn't. Come on, sweetheart, let's get a move on. You've got a game to pitch.'' The emphasis came on the last word. The first game of the season and Jeff had won the coveted position of first-string pitcher. Whether it was true or not, Jeff believed Cole's tutoring had given him the advantage over the competition. Jeff hadn't told him the news yet, keeping it a surprise for today.

"When you do see Cole, don't say anything, all right?'' Jeff pleaded as they headed toward the car. ''I want to be the one who tells him.''

"My lips are sealed,'' she said, holding up her right hand. For good measure, she pantomimed zipping her mouth closed. She slid into the car and started the engine, but she glanced in the rearview mirror several times, hoping Cole would somehow miraculously appear.

He didn't.

The game was scheduled for the baseball diamond in Balboa Park, which was less than two miles from Robin's house. A set of bleachers had been arranged around the diamonds, and Robin climbed to the top. It gave her an excellent view of the field—and of the parking lot.

Cole knew the game was at Balboa Park, but he didn't know which diamond and there were several. Depending on how late he was, he could waste valuable time looking for the right field.

The second inning had just begun when Heather Lawrence joined Robin. Robin smiled at her.

"Hi,'' Heather returned. ''What's the score?''

"Nothing nothing. It's the top of the second inning."

"How's the neighborhood Orel Hershiser doing?"

"Jeff's doing great. Terrific. He managed to keep his poise when the first batter got a hit off his second pitch. I think I took it worse than Jeff did."

Heather grinned and nodded. "It's the same way with me. Kelly played goalie for her soccer team last year, and every time the opposing team scored on her I took it like a bullet to the chest."

"Where's Kelly now?"

Heather motioned toward the other side of the field. The eight-year-old was leaning casually against a tall fir tree. "She didn't want Jeff to know she'd come to watch him. Her game was over a few minutes ago. They lost, but this is her first year and just about everyone else's, too. The game was more a comedy of errors than anything."

Robin laughed. It was thoughtful of her neighbor to stop by and see how Jeff's team was doing.

Heather laced her fingers over her knees. "Jeff's been talking quite a bit about Cole Camden." She made the statement sound more like a question and kept her gaze focused on the playing field.

"Oh?" Robin wasn't sure how to answer. "Cole was kind enough to give Jeff a few pointers about pitching techniques."

"Speaking of pitching techniques, you two certainly seem to be hitting it off."

Heather was beginning to sound a lot like Angela, who drilled her daily about her relationship with Cole, offering advice and unsolicited suggestions.

"I can't tell you how surprised I am at the changes I've seen in Cole since you two moved in. Kelly's been wanting to play in that fort from the moment she heard about it, but it's only since Jeff moved in that she was allowed in Cole's yard.''

"He's been good for Jeff," Robin said, training her eyes on the game. Cole's relationship with her son forced Robin to examine his motives. He'd lost a son, and there was bound to be a gaping hole in his heart. At first he hadn't allowed Jeff in his yard, or even approved of Blackie and Jeff's becoming friends. But without anything ever being said, all that had fallen to the wayside. Jeff played continually in Cole's yard, and with their neighbor's blessing. Jeff now had free access to the fort and often brought other neighborhood kids along with him. Apparently Cole had given permission. Did he consider Jeff a sort of substitute son? Robin shook off the thought.

"Jeff talks about Cole constantly," Heather said. "In fact, he told me this morning that Cole was coming to see him pitch. What happened? Did he get hung up at the office?"

"I don't know. He must have been delayed, but—"

"There he is! Over there." Heather broke in excitedly. "You know, in the two years we've lived on Orchard Street, I can only recall talking to Cole a handful of times. He was always so standoffish. Except when we were both doing yard work, I never saw him, and if we did happen to meet, we said hello and that was about it. The other day we bumped into each other at the grocery store and he actually smiled at me. I was stunned. I swear that's the first time I've ever seen that man smile. I honestly think you and Jeff are responsible for the change in him."

"I think you're crediting me with more than my due," Robin said, craning her head to look for Cole.

"No, I'm not," Heather argued. "You can't see the difference in him because you're new to the neighborhood, but everyone who's known him for any length of time will tell you he's like a different person."

Jeff was sitting on the bench while his team was up at bat. Suddenly he leapt to his feet and waved energetically several times, as though he was flagging down a rescue helicopter. His face broke into a wide, eager smile. His coach must have said something to him because Jeff nodded and took off running toward the parking lot.

Robin's gaze followed her son. Cole had indeed arrived. The tension eased out of her in a single breath. She hadn't realized how edgy she'd been. In her heart she realized Cole would never purposely disappoint Jeff, but her son's anxiety had been as keen as her own.

"Listen," Heather said, standing, "I'll talk to you later."

"Thanks for stopping by."

"Glad to," Heather said, climbing down the bleachers. She paused at the bottom and wiggled her eyebrows expressively, then laughed merrily at Robin's frown.

Heather must have passed Cole on her way out, but Robin lost sight of them as Jeff raced onto the pitcher's mound for the bottom of the second inning. Even from this distance Robin could see that his eyes were full of happy excitement. He discreetly shot her a look and Robin made a V-for-victory sign, smiling broadly.

Cole leapt up the bleachers and sat down beside her. "Sorry I'm late. I was trapped in a meeting, and by the time I could get out to phone you, you'd already left for the field."

"Jeff and I knew it was something like that."

"So he's pitching!" Cole's voice rang with pride.

"He claims it's all due to you."

"I'll let him believe that," Cole said, grinning, "but he's a natural athlete. All I did was teach him a little discipline and give him a means of practicing on his own."

"According to Jeff you taught him everything he knows."

He shook his head. "I'm glad I didn't miss the whole game."

"There'll be others," she said, but she was grateful he'd come when he had. From the moment they'd left the house, Robin had been tense and guarded. Cole could stand *her* up for any date, but disappointing Jeff was more than she could bear. Rarely had she felt this emotionally unsettled. And all because Cole had been late for a Balboa Park Baseball League game. It frightened her to realize how much Jeff was beginning to depend on him. And not just Jeff, either....

"This is important to Jeff," Cole said as if reading her mind, "and I couldn't disappoint him. If it had been anyone else it wouldn't have been nearly as important. But Jeff matters—" he paused and his eyes locked with hers "—and so do you."

Robin felt almost giddy with a flood of relief. For the first time since Lonny's tragic death, she understood how carefully, how completely, she'd anesthetized her life, refusing to admit anyone or anything into it that might cause her or Jeff more pain. For years she'd been drifting in a haze of denial and grief, refusing to acknowledge or deal with either. What Angela had said was true. Robin had dated infrequently and haphazardly, and kept any suitors at a safe and comfortable distance.

For some reason, she hadn't been able to do that with Cole. Robin couldn't understand what was different or why; all she knew was that she was in serious danger of falling for this man, and falling hard. It terrified her....

"Have you and Jeff had dinner?" Cole asked.

Robin turned to face him, but it was a long moment before she realized he'd asked her a question. He repeated it and she shook her head. "Jeff was too excited to eat."

"Good. There's an excellent Chinese restaurant close by. The three of us can celebrate after the game."

"That'd be nice," she whispered, thinking she should make some excuse to avoid this, and realizing almost immediately that she didn't want to avoid it at all.

"CAN I HAVE some more pork-fried rice?" Jeff asked.

Cole passed him the dish and Robin watched as her son heaped his plate high with a third helping.

"You won," she said wistfully.

"Mom, I wish you'd stop saying that. It's the fourth time you've said it. I know we won, you don't need to remind me," Jeff muttered, glancing at Cole as if to beg forgiveness for his mother, who was obviously suffering from an overdose of maternal pride.

"But Jeff, you were fantastic."

"The whole team was fantastic." Jeff reached for what was left of the egg rolls and added a dollop of plum sauce to his plate.

"I had no idea you were such a good hitter," Robin said, still amazed at her son's athletic ability. "I knew

you could pitch—I'd seen that myself. But two home
runs! Oh, Jeff, I'm so proud of you—and everyone
else." It was difficult to remember that Jeff was only
one member of a team, and that his success was part
of a larger effort.

"I wanted to make sure I played well, especially
'cause you were there, Cole." Once more Jeff
stretched his arm across the table, this time reaching
for the nearly empty platter of almond chicken.

As for herself, Robin couldn't down another bite.
Cole had said the food at the Golden Wok was good,
and he hadn't exaggerated. It was probably the best
Chinese meal she'd ever tasted. Jeff apparently
thought so, too. The boy couldn't seem to stop eating.

It was while they were laughing over their fortune
cookies that Robin heard bits and pieces of the conversation from the booth behind them.

"I bet they're celebrating something special," an
elderly gentleman commented.

"I think their little boy must have done well at the
baseball game," his wife said softly.

Their little boy, Robin mused. The older couple
dining directly behind them thought Cole and Jeff
were father and son.

Robin's eyes flew to Cole, but if he heard the comment, he didn't give any sign.

"His mother and father are certainly proud of
him."

"It's such a delight to see these young people so
happy. A family should spend time together."

A family. The three of them looked like a family.

Once more Robin glanced at Cole, but once again he seemed not to hear the comments. Or if he had, he ignored them.

But Cole must have sensed her scrutiny because his gaze found hers just then. Their eyes lingered without a hint of the awkwardness Robin had felt so often before.

Jeff chatted constantly on the ride home with Robin. Since they'd both brought their cars, they drove home separately. They exchanged good-nights in the driveway and entered their own houses.

Jeff had some homework to finish and Robin ran a load of clothes through the washing machine. An hour later, after a little television and quick baths, they were both ready for bed. Robin tucked the blankets around Jeff's shoulders, although he protested he was much too old for her to do that. But he didn't complain too loudly or too long.

"Night, Jeff."

"Night, Mom. Don't let the bedbugs bite."

"Don't go all sentimental on me, all right?" she teased, as she turned off his light. She was convinced he fell asleep the instant she left the room. She returned downstairs to secure the house for the night, then headed up to her own bedroom. Once upstairs, she paused in her son's doorway and smiled gently. They'd both had quite a day.

At about ten o'clock, she was sitting up in bed reading an Anne Perry mystery when the phone rang. She reached for it quickly, always anxious about late calls. "Hello."

"You're still awake." It was Cole, and his voice affected her like a surge of electricity.

"I . . . was reading," she said.

"It suddenly occurred to me that we never had the chance to finish our conversation the other night."

"What conversation?" Robin asked.

"The one at the front door...that Jeff interrupted. Remind me to give that boy lessons in timing, by the way."

"I don't even remember what we were talking about." She settled back against the pillows, savoring the sound of his voice, enjoying the small intimacy of lying in bed, listening to him. Her eyes drifted shut.

"As I recall you'd just said something about how it isn't any of your business who I lunch with or who I spend my weekends with. I assume you think I'm with a woman."

Robin's eyes shot open. "I can assure you, I don't think anything of the sort."

"I guess I should explain about the weekends."

"No. I mean, Cole, it really isn't my business. I can't believe I even suggested anything remotely like that. It doesn't matter. Really."

"I have some property north of here, about forty acres," he explained gently, despite her protests. "The land once belonged to my grandfather, and he willed it to me when he passed away a couple of years back. This house was part of the estate, as well. My father was born and raised here. I've been spending a good deal of my free time remodeling the old farmhouse. Sometime in the future, I might move out there."

"I see." She didn't want to think about Cole leaving the neighborhood, ever.

"The place still needs a lot of work, and I've enjoyed doing it on my own. It's coming along well."

She nodded and a second later realized he couldn't see the action. "It sounds lovely."

"Are there any other questions you'd like to ask me?" His voice was low and teasing.

"Of course not," she denied immediately.

"Then would you be willing to admit you enjoy it when I kiss you? A high seven? Really? I think Jeff's right—we need more practice."

"Uh..." Robin didn't know how to answer that.

"I'm willing," he said, and she could almost hear him smile.

Robin lifted the hair from her brow. "I can't believe we're having this discussion. I really can't."

"You said that before. Would it help if I told you how much I enjoy kissing you?"

"Please...don't," she whispered. She didn't want him to tell her that. Every time he kissed her, it confused her more. Despite the sheltered feeling she experienced in his arms, something deep and fundamental inside her was afraid of loving again. No, terrified. She was terrified of coming to care for Cole. Terrified of what the future might hold.

"The first time shook me more than I care to admit. Remember that Friday night we rented the movie?"

"I remember."

"I tried to stay away from you afterward. For an entire week I avoided you."

Robin didn't answer. She couldn't. Lying back against the pillows, she stared at the ceiling as a sense of warmth enveloped her. A feeling of comfort...of unfamiliar happiness.

There was a short silence, and in an effort to bring their discussion back to a less intimate—less risky—level, she said, "Thank you for dinner. Jeff had the time of his life." She had, too, but she couldn't find the courage to admit it.

"You're welcome."

"Are you going away this weekend to work on the property?"

She had no right to ask him that, and was shocked at how easily the question emerged.

"I don't think so." After another brief pause, he murmured, "When was the last time you went on a picnic and flew a kite?"

"I don't remember," she admitted.

"Would you consider going with me Saturday afternoon? You and Jeff. The three of us together."

"Yes...Jeff would love it."

"How about you? Would you love it?"

"Yes," she whispered.

There didn't seem to be anything more to say, and Robin ended the conversation. "I'll tell Jeff in the morning. He'll be thrilled. Thank you."

"I'll talk to you tomorrow then."

"Right. Tomorrow."

"Good night, Robin."

She smiled softly. He said her name the way she'd always dreamed a man would, softly, with a mixture of excitement and need. "Good night, Cole."

For a long time after they'd hung up Robin lay staring at her bedroom walls. When she did turn off her light, she fell asleep as quickly as Jeff seemed to have. She woke about midnight, surprised to find the sheets all twisted as if she'd tossed and turned frantically. The bedspread had slipped onto the floor, and the top sheet was wound around her legs, trapping her.

Sitting up, she untangled her legs and brushed the curls from her face, and wondered what had caused her restlessness. She didn't usually wake abruptly like this.

She slid off the bed, found her slippers and went downstairs for a glass of milk.

It was while she was sitting at the table that it came to her. Her hand stilled. Her heartbeat accelerated. The couple in the Chinese restaurant. Robin had overheard them and she was certain Cole must have, too.

Their little boy. A family.

Cole had lost a son. From what little Robin had learned, Cole's son had been about the same age as Jeff was now when he'd died. First divorce, and then death.

Suddenly it all made sense. A painful kind of sense. A panicky kind of sense. The common ground between them wasn't their backyards, but the fact that they were both victims.

Cole was trying to replace the family that had been so cruelly taken from him.

Robin was just as guilty. She had been so caught up in the tide of emotion and attraction that she'd refused to recognize what was staring her in the face. She'd ignored her own suspicions and fears, brushing them aside.

She and Cole were both hurting, needy people.

But once the hurt was assuaged, once the need had been satisfied, Cole would discover what Robin had known from the beginning. They were completely different people with little, if anything, in common.

CHAPTER SIX

"WHAT DO YOU MEAN you want to meet my cousin?" Angela demanded, glancing up from her desk, a shocked disbelieving look on her face.

"You've been after me for weeks to date Fred."

"Frank. Yes, I have, but that was B.C."

"B.C.?"

"Before Cole. What happened with you two?"

"Nothing!"

"And pigs have wings," Angela said with more than a trace of sarcasm. She stood up and walked around to the front of her desk, leaning against one corner while she folded her arms and stared unblinkingly at Robin.

Robin knew it would do little good to try to disguise her feelings. She'd had a restless night and was convinced it showed. No doubt her eyes were glazed; they ached. Her bones ached. But mostly her heart ached. Arranging a date with Angela's cousin was a sure indication of her distress.

"The last thing I heard, Cole was supposed to attend Jeff's baseball game with you."

"He did." Robin walked to her own desk and reached for the cup of coffee she'd brought upstairs with her. Peeling off the plastic lid, she cautiously took a sip.

"And?"

"Jeff pitched and he played a fabulous game," Robin supplied, hoping her friend wouldn't quiz her further.

Angela continued to stare at Robin. Good grief, Robin thought, the woman had eyes that could cut through solid rock. Superman should have eyes like this.

"What?" Robin demanded when she couldn't stand her friend's scrutiny any longer. She took another sip of her coffee and nearly scalded her lips. If the rest of her day followed the pattern set that morning, she might as well head home now. The temptation to climb back into bed and hide her head under the pillow was growing stronger every minute.

"Tell me what happened with Cole," Angela demanded.

"Nothing. I already told you he was at Jeff's baseball game. What more do you want?"

"The least you can do is tell me what went on last night," Angela said slowly, carefully enunciating each word as though speaking to someone who was hard of hearing.

"Before or after Jeff's baseball game?" Robin pulled out her chair and plopped herself down.

"Both."

Robin gave up. Gesturing weakly with her hands, she shrugged, took a deep breath and poured out the whole story in one huge rush. "Cole was held up at the office in a meeting, so we didn't meet at the house the way we'd planned. Naturally Jeff was disappointed, but we decided that whatever was keeping Cole wasn't his fault, and we left for Balboa Park without him. Cole arrived just as Jeff was ready to pitch the bottom of the second inning. Jeff only allowed three hits the entire game, and scored two home runs himself. Afterward Cole took us all out for Chinese food at a fabulous restaurant I've never heard of but one you and I will have to try sometime. Our next raise, okay? Later Cole phoned and asked to take Jeff and me on a picnic Saturday. I think we're going to Golden Gate Park because he also mentioned something about flying kites.'' She paused, dragged in a fresh gulp of air and gave Angela a look that said ''try and make something out of that!''

''I see,'' Angela said after a lengthy pause.

''Good.''

Robin wasn't up to explaining things, so if Angela really *didn't* understand, that was just too bad. She only knew that she was dangerously close to letting her emotions take charge of her life. She was becoming increasingly attracted to a man who could well be looking to replace the son he'd lost. Robin needed to find a way to keep from following her heart, which was moving at breakneck speed straight into Cole's arms.

''Will you introduce me to Frank or not?'' she demanded a second time, strengthening her voice and her conviction.

Angela continued to stare at her with those diamond-cutting eyes while she rubbed the sides of her jaw with her thumb and index finger. ''I'm not sure yet.''

''You're not sure!'' Robin echoed, dismayed. ''For weeks you've been spouting his virtues. According to you, this cousin is as near a god as a human being can get. He works hard, buys municipal bonds, attends church regularly and flosses his teeth.''

''I said all that?''

"Close enough," Robin muttered. "I made up the part about flossing his teeth. Yet when I ask to meet this paragon of limitless virtue, you say you're not sure you want to introduce me. I would have thought you'd be pleased."

"I am pleased," Angela said, frowning, "but I'm also concerned."

"It's not your job to be concerned. All you have to do is call Fred and let him know I'm available Saturday evening for drinks or dinner or a movie or whatever. I'll let him decide what he's most comfortable with."

"It's Frank, and I thought you just said you were going on a picnic with Cole on Saturday."

Robin unfolded a computer printout, prepared to check a long row of figures. If she looked busy and suitably nonchalant, it might prompt Angela into agreeing. "Jeff and I will be with Cole earlier in the day. I'll simply make sure we're back before late afternoon, so there's no reason to worry."

Robin's forehead puckered gently. "I am worried, I can't help being worried. Honestly, Robin, I've never seen you like this. You're so . . . so determined."

"I've always been determined," Robin countered, glancing up from the computer sheet.

"Oh, I agree one hundred percent," Angela said with a heavy sigh, "but not when it comes to anything that has to do with men. My thirteen-year-old niece has more savvy with the opposite sex than you do!"

"MOM, LOOK HOW HIGH my kite is," Jeff hollered as his box kite soared toward the heavens.

"It's touching the sky!" Robin shouted, and laughed with her son as he tugged and twisted the string. Despite all her misgivings about her relationship with Cole, she was thoroughly enjoying the afternoon. At first, she'd been convinced the day would turn into a disaster. She was sure Cole would take one look at her and know she was going out with another man that evening. She was equally sure she'd blurt it out if he didn't immediately guess.

Cole had been as excited as Jeff about the picnic and kite-flying expedition. The two of them had been fussing with the kites for hours—buying, building and now flying them. For her part, Robin was content to soak up the sunshine.

The weather couldn't have been more cooperative. The sky was as blue as she'd ever seen it and the wind was perfect. Sailboats scudding on the choppy green waters added dashes of bright color.

In contrast to all the beauty surrounding her, Robin's heart was troubled. Watching Cole, so patient and gentle with her son, filled her with contradictory emotions. Part of her wanted to thank him. Thank him for the smile that lit up Jeff's young face. Thank him for throwing open the shades and gently easing her toward the light. And part of her wanted to shut her eyes and run for cover.

"Mom, look!" Jeff cried as the kite whipped and kicked in the wind. Blackie raced at his side, as the sleek red-and-blue kite sliced through the sky, then dipped sharply and crashed toward the ground at heart-stopping speed, only to be caught at what seemed the last second and lifted higher and higher.

"I'm looking, I'm looking!" Robin shouted back. She'd never seen Jeff happier. Pride and joy shone from his face, and Robin was moved almost to tears.

Cole stood behind Jeff, watching the kite. One hand rested on the boy's shoulder, the other shaded his eyes as he gazed toward the sky. The two laughed, and once more Robin was struck by the mingling of their voices. One mature and measured, the other young and excited. Both happy.

A few moments later, Cole jogged over to Robin's blanket and sat down beside her. He did nothing more than smile at her, but she felt an almost physical jolt.

Cole stretched out and leaned back on his elbows, grinning at the sun. "I can't remember the last time I laughed so much."

"You two certainly seem to be enjoying this," Robin said.

If Cole noticed anything awry with her, he didn't comment. She'd managed not to tell him about the date with Angela's cousin; she certainly didn't want him to think she was trying to make him jealous. That wasn't the evening's purpose at all. Actually she wasn't sure she fully understood *what* she hoped to accomplish by dating Fred... Frank. She mentally shouted the name five times. Why ever did she keep calling him Fred? She didn't know that any more than she knew why she was going out with him. On the morning she'd talked Angela into making the arrangements for her, it had seemed a matter of life and death. Now she only felt confused and regretful.

"Jeff says you've got a date this evening."

So much for her worry that she might blurt it out herself, Robin thought. She glanced at Cole. He might have been referring to a minor rise in stock prices for all the emotion revealed in his voice.

"A cousin of a good friend. She's been after me for months to meet Frank—we're having dinner."

"Could this be the Frank you weren't going out with and that was final?"

Robin stared at him blankly.

"You answered the phone with that when I called to inquire about Blackie. Remember?"

"Oh, yes," she muttered. Suddenly she felt an intense need to justify her actions. "It's just that Angela's been talking about him for so long and it seemed like the right thing to do. He's apparently very nice and Angela's been telling me that he's a lot of fun and I didn't think it would hurt to meet him...." Once she got started, Robin couldn't seem to stop explaining.

"Robin," Cole said gently, his eyes tender. "You don't owe me any explanations."

She instantly grew silent. He was right, she knew that, yet she couldn't help feeling guilty and confused. She was making a terrible mess of this.

"I'm not the jealous type," Cole informed her matter-of-factly.

"I'm not trying to make you jealous," she returned stiffly.

"Good," Cole said and shrugged. His gaze moved from her to Jeff who was jogging across the grass. Blackie was at his side, barking excitedly.

He hadn't asked, but she felt obliged to explain who would be watching her son while she was out. "Jeff's going to the movies with Heather and Kelly Lawrence while I'm out."

Cole didn't say anything. All he did was smile. It was the same smile he'd flashed at her earlier. The same devastating, wickedly charming smile.

He seemed to be telling her that she could dine with a thousand different men and it wouldn't disturb him in the least. As he said, he wasn't the jealous type. Great. This was exactly the way she'd wanted him to respond, wasn't it? She could date a thousand different men, because Cole didn't care about her. He cared about her son.

"Let me know when you want to leave," he said with infuriating self-assurance. "I wouldn't want you to be late."

On that cue, Robin checked her watch and was surprised to note that it was well past four. They'd been having so much fun, the day had simply slipped away. When she looked up, she found Cole watching her expectantly. "It's...I'm not meeting Frank until later," she said, answering his unspoken question evasively while she gathered up the remains of their picnic.

It was an hour later when they decided to leave Golden Gate Park. Jeff and Cole loaded up the kites, as well as the picnic cooler, and placed them in the back of Cole's car. It took them nearly an hour to get back to Glen Park because of the heavy traffic, which pinched Robin's schedule even more tightly. But that was hardly Cole's fault—it wasn't as if he'd *arranged* for an accident on the freeway.

Cole and Jeff chatted easily for most of the ride home. Sitting in the back, Jeff leaned so far forward his face was poised directly between Robin and Cole.

When they arrived at the house, both Robin and Jeff helped Cole unload the car. Blackie's barking only added to the confusion.

"I suppose I'd better get into the house," Robin said, her eyes briefly meeting Cole's. She felt awkward all of a sudden, wishing Jeff was there as a barrier, instead of carting things onto Cole's porch.

"We had a great time," she added self-consciously. She couldn't really blame her nervousness on Cole; he'd been the perfect companion all day. "Thank you for the picnic."

Jeff joined them, his eyes narrowing as he looked at Cole. "Are you honestly going to let her do it?"

"Do what?" Robin demanded of her son.

"Go out with that other man," Jeff said righteously, inviting Cole to leap into the argument. "I can't believe you're going to let her get away with this."

"Jeff. This isn't something we should be discussing with Mr. Camden."

"All right," he murmured with an expressive sigh. "But I think you're making a mistake." He cast a speculative glance in Cole's direction. "Both of you," he mumbled under his breath and headed for the house.

"Thanks for the wonderful afternoon, Cole," Robin said again.

"No problem," he answered, hands in his pockets, his stance relaxed. "Have a good time with Frank."

"Thanks, I will," she muttered, squinting at him suspiciously just before she turned toward the house. Darn it, she actually felt guilty! There wasn't a single solitary reason she should feel guilty for agreeing to this dinner date with Angela's cousin, yet she did. Cole must have known it, too, otherwise he wouldn't have made that remark about having a good time. Oh, he knew all right.

As Robin was running the bath, Jeff raced up the stairs. "Mom, I need money for the movie." He thrust her purse into her hands. "How much are you going to give me for goodies?"

"Goodies?"

"You know popcorn, pop, a couple of candy bars. I'm starving."

"Jeff, you haven't stopped eating all day. What about the two hot dogs I just fixed you?"

"I ate them, but that was ten or fifteen minutes ago. I'm hungry again."

Robin handed him seven dollars, prepared for an argument. That amount was enough to pay his way into the movie and supply him with popcorn and a soda. Anything beyond that he could do without.

Jeff took the money from her and slowly shook his head, as though she'd intentionally slighted him. "That's it, kid," she said in a firm voice.

"Did I complain?" Bright blue eyes stared back at her innocently.

"You didn't have to. I could see the rebellion in your face."

Jeff was ready to leave a few minutes later, just as Robin was getting dressed. He stood outside her bedroom door and shouted that Kelly and her mom were there to pick him up.

"Have a good time. I won't be later than ten-thirty," she assured him.

"Can't I wait for you over at Cole's after the movie?"

"Absolutely not!" Robin's heart skidded to a dead stop at the suggestion. The last person she wanted to face at the end of this evening was Cole Camden. "You didn't ask him, did you?"

"No... but I'm not all that excited about going to Kelly's afterward. I'm there every day, you know."

"Sweetie, I'm sorry. I promise I won't be late."

"You're sure I can't go over to Cole's?"

"Jeffrey Leonard Masterson, don't you dare bother Cole, do you understand me?"

He blinked a couple of times. She rarely used that tone of voice with him, but she didn't have the time or energy to argue about this.

"I guess," he said with an exaggerated sigh. "But could you make it home closer to ten?"

"Why ten?"

"Because I don't want to do anything stupid like fall asleep in front of Kelly," he whispered heatedly.

"I'll be back as soon as I can," Robin promised.

Glancing at her clock radio, she gasped at the time. She was running late. From the moment she'd made the arrangements to meet Frank, she hadn't given the reality of this evening much thought. Just forcing herself to go through with it had depleted her of energy.

Robin had always hated situations like this. Always. She was going to a strange restaurant, meeting a strange man, and for what? She didn't know.

Tucking her feet into her pumps, Robin hurried to the bathroom to spray on a little cologne. Not much, just enough to give herself some confidence. She rushed down the stairs and reached for her purse.

Her hand was on the doorknob when the phone rang. For a moment, Robin intended to ignore it. It was probably for Jeff. But what if the call was from her parents? Or Frank—calling to cancel? Ridiculous though it was, each ring sounded more urgent than the last. She'd just have to answer, or she'd wonder who it was all evening. Muttering under her breath, she dashed into the kitchen.

"Hello," she said impatiently.

For a moment there was no response. "Robin, it's Cole." He sounded nothing like himself. "I lied." With that the line was abruptly disconnected.

Robin held the receiver away from her ear and stared at it for several seconds. He'd lied? About what? Good heavens, why had he even phoned? To tell her he'd lied.

There wasn't time to phone him back and ask what he meant.

"WOULD YOU CARE for something to drink?" Frank Eberle asked, glancing over the wine list.

"Nothing, thanks," Robin said. Frank had turned out to be a congenial sort, which was a pleasant surprise. He was quite attractive, with light blue eyes and a thick head of distinguished-looking salt-and-pepper hair. Angela had once mentioned he was "a little bit" shy, which had panicked Robin since she was a whole lot shy, at least around men. The way she'd figured it, they'd stare at each other most of the night, not knowing what to say. At least they had Angela in common. Whereas with Cole, all they shared was—

Her thoughts came to an abrupt stop. She refused to think about her neighbor or his last-minute phone call. She balked at the idea of dining with one man and wistfully longing for another—which was exactly what she was doing.

Robin studied the menu, pretending to decide between the prime-rib special and the fresh halibut. But the entire time she gazed at the menu, she was racking her brain for a topic of conversation.

Frank saved her the trouble. "For once," he said, "Angela didn't exaggerate. You're something of a surprise."

"I am?" It was amusing to hear him echo her own reaction.

Frank nodded, his smile gentle and reserved. "When Angie phoned earlier in the week, I wasn't sure what to expect. She keeps wanting me to date her friends. And to hear her talk, she's close friends with dozens of gorgeous women all interested in meeting me."

Robin grinned. "She should run a dating service. I can't tell you the number of times she's matched me up with someone, or at least tried to."

"But you're a comfortable kind of person to be around. I could sense that right away."

"Thank you. I...wasn't sure what to expect, either. Angela's raved about you for weeks, wanting to get the two of us together." Robin glanced from the menu to her companion, then back again. She felt the same misgivings every time she agreed to one of these arranged dates.

"I've been divorced six months now," Frank volunteered, "but after fourteen years of married life, I don't think I'll ever get accustomed to dating again."

Robin found herself agreeing. "I know what you mean. It all seems so awkward, doesn't it? When Lonny and I were dating I was in high school, and there was so little to consider. We knew what we wanted and knew what we had to do to get there."

Frank gave her a small smile. "Now that we're older and—" he paused "—I hesitate to use the word wiser...."

"More sophisticated?"

"Right, more sophisticated," Frank repeated. His hand closed around the water glass. "Life is so complicated now. I'd been out of the swing of things for so long, I hadn't realized that the role men played in relationships had changed. Women aren't the fragile creatures they used to be, if you know what I mean."

Robin had certainly been feeling fragile and artless and incredibly naive, but she nodded. "Men aren't the same, either."

"You're right about that," Frank said with an abrupt nod of his head.

The waitress came for their order, and from then on the evening went smoothly. The sense of kinship she felt with Frank surprised Robin. He was obviously at ease, too. Before she knew how it happened, Robin found herself telling him about Cole.

"He sounds like the kind of guy most women would leap off a bridge to meet."

Robin nodded. "He's wonderful to Jeff, too."

"Then what's the problem."

"His wife and son."

Frank's mouth sagged open. "He's married?"

"Was," she rushed to explain. "From what I understand his wife left him and sometime later his son died."

"That's tough," Frank said, reaching for his coffee. "But that was years ago, right?"

"I...don't know. Cole's never told me these things himself. In fact, he's never mentioned either his wife or his son."

"He's never mentioned them?"

"Never," she confirmed. "I heard it from a neighbor."

"That's what's bothering you, isn't it?"

The question was sobering. Subconsciously, from the moment Robin had learned of Cole's loss, she'd been waiting for him to tell her. Waiting for him to trust her enough. Waiting for him to share his pain.

Frank and Robin lingered over coffee, chatting about politics and the economy and several other stimulating topics. But the question about Cole refused to fade from her mind.

They parted outside the restaurant and Frank kissed her cheek, but they were both well aware they wouldn't be seeing each other again. Their time together had been a brief respite. It had helped Frank deal with his loneliness and helped Robin understand what was troubling her about Cole.

The first thing Robin noticed when she pulled into her driveway was that Cole's house was dark. Dark and silent. Silent and lonely. So much of her life had been those things—before she'd met him.

She needed to talk to him. She wanted to ask him about his phone call. She longed to ask him about his wife and the son he'd lost. But the timing was all wrong.

For a long moment Robin sat alone in her car feeling both disappointed and sad.

Heather greeted her with a smile and a finger pressed to her lips. "Both kids were exhausted. They fell asleep in the living room almost as soon as we got back."

After Jeff's busy day, it was astonishing that he'd lasted through the movie. "I hope he wasn't cranky."

"Not in the least," Heather assured her.

Robin yawned, and realized how exhausted she was. She wanted nothing more than to escape to her room and sleep until noon the following day.

"Would you like a cup of coffee before you go?" Heather asked.

"No, thanks." Robin had been blessed with good neighbors. Heather on her right and Cole on her left.

Together Robin and Heather woke Jeff, who grumbled about his mother being late. He was too drowsy to realize it was only nine-thirty, or that she'd returned ahead of schedule.

After telling Heather a little about her evening, Robin guided her son across the yard and into the house. She walked upstairs with him and answered the slurred questions he struggled to ask between wide, mouth-stretching yawns.

Tugging back his comforter, Robin gently urged him into his bed. Jeff kicked off his shoes and reached for the quilt. It wasn't the first time he'd slept in his clothes and it probably wouldn't be the last.

Smiling to herself, Robin quietly moved down the stairs.

On impulse, she paused in the kitchen and reached for the phone. When Cole answered on the first ring, she swallowed a gasp of surprise.

"Hello," he said a second time.

"What did you lie about?" she asked softly.

"Where are you?"

"Home."

"I'll be right there." Without a further word, he hung up.

A minute later, Cole was standing at her front door, hands in his back pockets. He stared at her as if it had been months since they'd last seen each other.

"All right, you win," he said, edging his way in.

"Win what? The door prize?" she asked, controlling her amusement with difficulty.

Not bothering to answer her, Cole headed for the kitchen, where he sank down in one of the pine chairs. "Did you have a good time?"

She sat down across from him. "I really did. Frank's a gentle, caring man. We met at the Higher Ground—that's a cute little restaurant close to the BART station and—"

"I know where it is."

"About your phone call earlier. You said—"

"What's he like?"

"Who? Frank?"

Cole gave her a look that suggested she have her intelligence tested.

"He's very nice. Divorced and lonely."

"What's he do for a living?"

"He works for the city, I think. We didn't get around to talking about our careers." No doubt Cole would be shocked if he knew she'd spent the greater part of the evening discussing her relationship with him!

"What did you talk about then?"

"Cole, honestly, I don't think we should discuss my evening with Frank. Would you like some coffee?"

"Are you going to see him again?"

Robin ignored the question. Instead she left the table and began to make coffee. She was concentrating so carefully on her task that she didn't notice Cole was directly behind her. She turned—and found herself gazing into the darkest, most confused and frustrated pair of eyes she'd ever seen.

"Oh," she gasped. "I didn't realize you were so close."

His hands gripped her shoulders. "Why did you go out with him?"

Surely that wasn't distress she heard in Cole's voice. Not after all that casual indifference this afternoon. She frowned, bewildered by the weary pain she saw in his eyes. And she finally realized: contrary to everything he'd claimed, Cole was jealous. Really truly jealous.

"Did he kiss you?" He asked the question with an urgency, an intensity, she'd never heard in his voice before.

Robin blinked, frozen by the stark need she read in him.

Cole's finger rested on her mouth. "Did Frank kiss you?" he repeated.

She shook her head and the motion brushed his finger across the fullness of her bottom lip.

"He wanted to, though, didn't he?" Cole asked with a brooding frown.

"He didn't kiss me." She was finally able to say the words. She couldn't kiss Frank, or anyone else. The only man she wanted to be kissed and held by was the man looking down at her now. The man whose lips were descending on hers . . .

CHAPTER SEVEN

"SO, DID YOU LIKE this guy you had dinner with last night?" Jeff asked, keeping his eyes on his bowl of cold cereal.

"He was nice," Robin answered, pouring herself a cup of coffee and joining him at the table. They'd slept late and were spending a lazy Sunday morning enjoying their breakfast before heading for the eleven o'clock service at church.

Jeff hesitated, his spoon poised above the bowl. "Is he nicer than Cole?"

"Cole's . . . nicer," Robin admitted reluctantly. "Nice" and "nicer" weren't terms she would have used to describe the differences between Frank and Cole, but in her son's ten-year-old mind they made perfect sense.

A smile quivered at the edges of Jeff's mouth. "I saw you two smooching last night," he said, grinning broadly.

"When?" Robin demanded—a ridiculous question. It could only have been when Cole had come over to talk to her. He'd admitted how jealous he'd been of Frank and how he'd struggled with the emotion and felt like a fool. Robin had been convinced she was the one who'd behaved like a dolt. Before either of them could prevent it, they were in each other's arms, seeking and granting reassurance.

"You thought I was asleep, but I heard Cole talking and I wanted to ask him what he was going to do about you dating this other guy; so I came downstairs and saw you two with your faces stuck together."

The boy certainly had a way with words.

"You didn't look like you minded, either. Cole and me talked about girls once and he said they aren't much when they're ten or so, but they get a whole lot more interesting later on. He said girls are like green apples. At first they're all sour and make your lips pucker, but a little while later, they're real good."

"I see," Robin muttered, not at all certain she liked being compared to an apple.

"But when I got down the stairs I didn't say anything," Jeff said, "because, well, you know."

Robin nodded and sipped her coffee in an effort to disguise her discomfort.

Jeff picked up his cereal bowl and drank the remainder of the milk in loud gulps. He wiped the back of his hand across his lips. "I suppose this means you're going to have a baby now."

Robin was too horrified to speak. The swallow of coffee caught halfway down her throat and she started choking. In an effort to help her breathe, Jeff started pounding her back with his fist, which only added to her misery.

By the time she caught her breath, the tears were streaking down her face.

"You all right, Mom?" Jeff asked, his eyes wide with concern. He rushed into the bathroom and returned with a wad of tissue.

"Thanks," she whispered, wiping her face. It took her a moment or two to regain her composure. This was a talk she'd planned on having with her son a few years down the road. "Jeff, listen . . . kissing doesn't make babies."

"It doesn't? But I thought . . . I'd hoped . . . You mean you won't be having a baby?"

"I . . . Not from kissing," she whispered, taking in deep breaths to stabilize her pulse.

"I suppose the next thing you're going to tell me is that we'll have to save up for a baby the way we did for the house and now the fence before we get me a dog."

This conversation was growing more complicated by the moment. "No, we wouldn't have to save for a baby."

"Then what's the holdup?" her son demanded. "I like the idea of being a big brother. I didn't think much about it until we moved here. Then when we were having dinner at the Chinese restaurant I heard this grandma and grandpa couple in the booth next to us talking, and they were saying neat things about us being a family. That was when I started thinking real serious about babies and stuff."

"Jeff," Robin said, rubbing her hands together as she gathered her thoughts. "It isn't as simple as that. Before there's a baby, there should be a husband."

"Well, of course," Jeff returned, looking at her as if she'd insulted his intelligence. "You'd have to marry Cole first, but that would be all right with me. You like him, don't you? You must, otherwise you wouldn't be kissing him that way."

Robin sighed. Of course she *liked* Cole, but it wasn't that simple. Unfortunately she wasn't sure she could explain it in terms a ten-year-old could understand. "I—"

"I can't remember ever seeing you kiss a guy like that. You looked real serious. And when I was sneaking back up the stairs I heard him ask you to have dinner alone with him tonight and that seemed like a real good sign, if you know what I mean.''

The next time Cole kissed her, Robin thought wryly, they'd have to scurry to a closet out of Jeff's view. The things that child came up with . . .

''You are going to dinner with him, aren't you?''

''Yes, but—''

''Then what's the problem? I'll ask him to marry you if you want.''

''Jeff!'' she cried, leaping to her feet. ''Absolutely not. That's something between Cole and me, and neither of us would appreciate any assistance from you. Is that clearly understood?''

''All right,'' he muttered, but he didn't look too pleased. He reached for a piece of toast, shredding it into thirds. ''But you're going to marry him, aren't you?''

''I don't know.''

''Why not? Cole's the best thing that's happened to us.''

Her son was staring at her intently, his baseball cap twisted around to the back of his head. Now that she had his full attention, Robin couldn't find the words to explain. ''There's more to it than you realize, sweetie.'' She made a show of glancing at the clock. ''It's time to change and get ready for church.''

Jeff nodded and rushed up the stairs. Robin followed at a much slower pace, grateful to put an end to this complicated and embarrassing subject.

The minute they were home from the service, Jeff reached for his baseball mitt. ''Jimmy Wallach and I are going to the school yard to practice hitting balls. Okay?''

"Okay," Robin said absently. "How long will you be gone?"

"An hour."

"I'm going grocery shopping, so if I'm not home when you get back, you know what to do?"

"Of course," he muttered.

"YOU'RE ROBIN MASTERSON, aren't you?" a tall middle-aged woman asked as she manipulated her grocery cart alongside of Robin's.

"Yes," Robin said expectantly. The other woman's eyes were warm and her smile friendly.

"I thought you must be—I've seen you from a distance. I'm Joyce Wallach. Jimmy and Jeff are good friends. In fact they're at the school yard now, hitting baseballs."

"Of course," Robin said, pleased to make the other woman's acquaintance. They'd talked on the phone several times, and she'd met Joyce's husband once, when Jimmy had spent the night. The boys had wanted to play on the same baseball team and were keenly disappointed when they'd been assigned to different teams. It had been Jimmy who'd told Jeff about the death of Cole's son.

"I've been meaning to invite you to the house for coffee," Joyce went on to say, "but I started working part-time and I can't seem to get myself organized."

"I know what you mean." Working full-time, keeping up with Jeff and her home was about all Robin could manage herself. She didn't know how other mothers were able to accomplish so much.

"There's a place to sit down here," Joyce said, and her eyes brightened with the idea. "Do you have time to chat now?"

Robin agreed, delighted. "Sure. I've been wanting to meet you, too." The Wallachs lived two streets over, and Robin fully approved of Jimmy as a friend for Jeff. He and Kelly had become friends, too, but her ten-year-old son wasn't as eager to admit being buddies with a girl. Kelly was still a green apple in Jeff's eye, but the time would come when he'd appreciate having her next door.

"I understand Jeff's quite the baseball player," Joyce said at the self-serve counter.

Robin nodded. She poured herself a plastic cup of iced tea and paid for it. "Jeff really loves baseball. He was disappointed he couldn't play with Jimmy."

"They separate the teams according to the year of birth. Jimmy's birthday is in January so he's with another group." She frowned. "That doesn't really make much sense, does it?" She chuckled, and Robin couldn't help responding to the soft infectious sound of Joyce's laughter. She found herself laughing, too.

They pulled out chairs at one of the small tables in the supermarket's deli section.

"I feel like throwing my arms around you," Joyce said, grinning broadly. "I happened to see Cole Camden the other day and I couldn't believe my eyes. It was like seeing him ten years ago, the way he used to be. I thought I saw Jeff with him. Did the two of them happen to be at Balboa Park recently?"

"Cole came to Jeff's first game."

"Ah." She nodded, as if that explained it. "I don't know if anyone's told you, but there's been a marked difference in Cole lately. I can't tell you how happy I am to see it. Cole's gone through so much heartache."

"Cole's been wonderful for Jeff," Robin said, then swallowed tightly. She felt a renewed stab of fear that Cole was more attracted to the idea of having a son than he was in a relationship with her.

"I have the feeling you've *both* been wonderful for him," Joyce added.

Robin's smile was losing its conviction. She lowered her gaze and studied the lemon slice floating on top of her tea.

"My husband and I knew Cole quite well before the divorce," Joyce went on to explain. "Larry, that's my husband, and Cole played golf every Saturday afternoon. Then Janice decided she wanted out of the marriage, left him and took Bobby. Cole really tried to save that marriage, but the relationship had been in trouble for a good long while. Cole doted on his son, though—he would have done anything to spare Bobby the trauma of a divorce. Janice, however—" Joyce halted abruptly, apparently realizing how much she'd said. "I didn't mean to launch into all this—it's ancient history. I just wanted you to know how pleased I am to meet you at last."

Since Cole had told her shockingly little of his past, Robin had to bite her tongue not to plead with Joyce to continue. Instead, she bowed her head and said, "I'm pleased to meet you, too."

Then she looked up with a smile. "Jimmy's finally got the friend he's always wanted. There are so few boys his age around here. I swear my son was ready to set off firecrackers the day Jeff registered at the school and he learned you lived only two blocks away."

"Jeff claimed he couldn't live in a house that's surrounded by girls." Robin shook her head with a mock grimace. "If he hadn't met Jimmy, I might have had a mutiny on my hands."

Joyce's face relaxed into a warm smile. She was energetic, animated and fun, gesturing freely with her hands as she spoke. Robin felt as if she'd known and liked Jimmy's mother for years.

"There hasn't been much turnover in this neighborhood over the years. We're a close-knit group, as I'm sure you've discovered. Heather Lawrence is a real sweetie. I wish I had more time to get to know her. And Cole, well . . . I realize that huge house has been in his family for years, but I half expected him to move out after Janice and Bobby were killed."

The silence that followed was punctuated by Robin's soft involuntary gasp. "What did you just say?"

"That I couldn't understand why Cole continued living in the house on Orchard Street. Is that what you mean?"

"No, after that—about Janice and Bobby." It was difficult for Robin to speak. Her tongue was desert dry and each word felt as if it had been scraped from the roof of her mouth.

"I assumed you knew they'd both been killed," Joyce said, her eyes full of concern. "I didn't realize, I mean, I thought for sure that Cole had told you."

"I knew about Bobby. Jimmy said something to Jeff, and Jeff told me, but I hadn't any idea that Janice had died, too. Heather Lawrence told me about the divorce, but she didn't say anything about Cole's wife dying."

"I don't think Heather knows. She moved into the neighborhood long after the divorce, and Lord knows Cole's close-mouthed enough about it."

"When did all this happen?"

"Several years ago now. It was all terribly tragic," Joyce said. "Just thinking about it makes my heart ache all over again. I don't mean to be telling tales, but frankly if there's any blame to be placed, I'm afraid it would fall on Janice. She wasn't the kind of woman who's easy to know or like. I shouldn't speak ill of the dead, and I don't mean to be catty, but Janice did Cole a favor when she left him. Naturally, he didn't see it that way—he was in love with his wife and crazy about his son. Frankly, I think Cole turned a blind eye to his wife's faults because of Bobby."

"What happened?" Perhaps having a neighbor fill in the details of Cole's life was the wrong thing to do; Robin no longer knew. Cole had never said a word to her about Janice or Bobby, and she didn't know if he ever would.

"Janice was never satisfied with Cole's position as a city attorney," Joyce explained. "We'd have coffee together every now and then, and all she'd do was complain how Cole was wasting his talents and that he could be making big money and wasn't. She had bigger plans for him. But Cole loved his job and felt an obligation to follow through with his commitments. Janice never understood that. She didn't even try to sympathize with Cole's point of view. She constantly wanted more, better, newer things. She didn't work herself, you know.

"Janice was never happy, never satisfied. She hated the house and the neighborhood, but she soon realized all the whining and manipulating in the world wasn't going to do one bit of good. Cole fully intended to finish out his responsibilities to the city, so she played her ace. She left him, taking Bobby with her."

"But didn't Cole try to gain custody of Bobby?"

"Of course. He knew, and so did everyone else, that Janice was using their son as a pawn. She was never the motherly type, if you know what I mean. If you want the truth, Janice was an alcoholic. There were several times I dropped Bobby off at the house and suspected Janice had been drinking heavily. I was willing to testify on Cole's behalf, and I told him so. He was grateful, but then the accident happened and it was too late."

"The accident?" A huge heaviness settled in her chest. Each breath pained her and brought with it the memories she longed to forget, memories of another accident—the one that had taken her husband from her.

"It was Janice's fault—the accident, I mean. She'd been drinking and should never have been behind the wheel of a car. The day before, Cole had been in to see his attorneys, pleading with them to move quickly because he feared Janice was becoming more and more irresponsible. But it wasn't until after Janice moved out that Cole realized how sick she'd become, how dependent she was on alcohol to make it through the day."

"Dear Lord," Robin whispered. "Cole must have felt so guilty."

"It was terrible," Joyce returned, her voice quavering. "I didn't know if Cole would survive that first year. He holed up inside the house and severed relationships with everyone in the neighborhood. He was consumed by his grief. Later he seemed to come out of it a little, but he's never been the same.

"The irony of all this is that eventually Janice would have got all she wanted, had she been more patient. A couple of years ago, Cole accepted a partnership in one of the most important law firms in the city. He's made a real name for himself, but money and position don't seem to mean much to him—they never have. I wouldn't be surprised if he walked away from the whole thing someday.''

''I think you're right. Cole told me not long ago that he has some property north of here that he inherited from his grandfather. He's restoring the house, and he said something about moving there. It's where he spends most of his weekends.''

''I wondered if it was something like that,'' Joyce said, nodding. ''There were rumors floating around the neighborhood that he spent his weekends with a woman. Anyone who knew Cole would realize what a crock that is. Cole isn't the type to have a secret affair.''

Robin felt ashamed, remembering how she'd been tempted to believe the rumor herself.

''For a long time,'' Joyce went on, ''I wondered if Cole was ever going to recover from Janice and Bobby's deaths, but now I believe he has. I can't help thinking you and Jeff have had a lot to do with that.''

''I...think he would have come out of his shell eventually.''

''Perhaps, but the changes in him lately have been the most encouraging things so far. I don't know how you feel about Cole or if there's anything between you, but you couldn't find a better man.''

''I...I'm falling in love with him,'' Robin whispered, voicing her feelings for the first time. The words hung in the air like a dark, heavy cloud.

''But I think that's absolutely wonderful, I really do!'' Joyce said enthusiastically.

"I don't." Now that the shock had worn off, Robin was forced to confront her anger. Cole had told her none of this. Not a single word. That hurt. Hurt more than she could have expected. But the ache she felt was nothing compared to the grief Cole must face each morning, the pain that weighed down his life.

"Oh, dear," Joyce said. "I've really done it now, haven't I? I knew I should have kept my mouth shut. You're upset and it's my fault."

"Nonsense," Robin whispered, making an effort to bring a smile to her dry lips and not succeeding. "I'm grateful we met, and more than grateful you told me about Janice, and about Cole's son." The knowledge produced a dull ache in Robin's heart. She felt grief for Cole and a less worthy emotion, too—a sense of being slighted by his lack of trust in her.

She was so upset on the short drive home that she missed the turn onto Orchard Street and had to take a side street and double back.

As she neared the house, she saw that Cole was outside watering his lawn. He waved, but she pretended not to notice and pulled into the driveway. Desperate for some time alone before facing Cole, Robin did her best to ignore him as she climbed out of the car. She needed a few more minutes to gather her thoughts and tutor her emotions.

She was almost safe, almost at the house, when Cole stopped her.

"Robin," he called, jogging toward her. "Hold on a minute, would you?"

She managed to compose herself, squaring her shoulders and drawing on her dignity.

His wonderful eyes were smiling as he hurried across over, fast approaching her. Obviously he hadn't realized there was anything wrong. "Did Jeff happen to say anything to you about seeing us kiss last night?" he asked.

Her mouth was so dry, she had to swallow a couple of times before she could utter a single syllable. "Yes, but don't worry, I think I've got him squared away."

"Drat!" he teased, snapping his fingers. "I suppose this means I don't have to go through with the shotgun wedding?"

She nodded, keeping her eyes lowered, fearing he would be able to read all the emotion churning inside her.

"You have nothing to fear but fear itself," she said, forcing a lightness into her tone.

"Robin?" He made her name a question and a caress. "Is something wrong?"

She shook her head, shifting the bag of groceries from one arm to the other. "Of course not," she said with the same feigned cheerfulness.

Cole lifted the bag from her arms. Robin knew she should have resisted, but she couldn't; she felt drained of strength. She headed for the house, knowing Cole would follow her inside.

"What's wrong?" he asked a second time, setting the groceries on the kitchen counter.

It was still difficult to speak and even more difficult, more exhausting, to find the words that would explain what she'd learned.

"Nothing. It's just that I've got a lot to do if we're going out for dinner tonight."

"Wear something fancy. I'm taking you to a four-star restaurant."

"Something fancy?" Mentally she reviewed the contents of her closet, which was rather lacking in fancy.

"I'm not about to be outclassed by Frank," Cole teased. "I'm going to wine and dine you and turn your head with sweet nothings."

He didn't need to do any of those things to turn her head. She was already dangerously close to being in love with him, so close that she'd blurted it out to a woman she'd known for a grand total of twelve minutes.

Abruptly switching her attention to the bag of groceries, Robin set several packages on the counter. When Cole's hands settled over her shoulders, her eyes drifted shut. "It isn't necessary," she found herself admitting.

Cole turned her around to face him. "What isn't?"

"The dinner, the wine, the sweet nothings."

Their gazes held. As if choreographed, they moved into each other's arms. With a groan that came deep from in his throat, Cole kissed her. His hands tangled in the auburn thickness of her hair. His lips closed over hers with fierce protectiveness.

Robin curled her arms tightly around his neck as her own world started to dip and spin and whirl. She was standing on her tiptoes, her heart in her throat, when she heard the front door open.

Moaning, she dragged her mouth from Cole's and broke away just as Jeff strolled into the kitchen.

The ten-year-old stopped, his brow furrowed, when he saw the two of them in what must surely look like suspicious circumstances.

"Hi, Mom. Hi, Cole." He strolled casually to the refrigerator and yanked open the door. "Is there anything decent to drink around this place?"

"Water?" Robin suggested.

Jeff rolled his eyes. "Funny, Mom, real funny."

"There are a few more sacks of groceries in the car. Would you get them for me?" He tossed her a look that suggested the child-labor laws needed reviewing, until Robin added, "You'll find a six-pack of soda in there."

"Okay." He raced out of the house and returned a minute later, carrying one sack and sorting through its contents as he walked slowly into the kitchen.

"I'll lend you a hand, sport," Cole said, placing his hand on Jeff's shoulder. He glanced at Robin and his eyes told her they'd continue their discussion at a more opportune moment.

Robin started emptying the sacks, hardly paying attention as Jeff and Cole brought in the last couple of bags. Cole told her he'd pick her up at six, then left.

"Can I play with Blackie for a while?" Jeff asked, a can of cold soda clenched in his hand.

"All right," Robin answered, grateful to have a few minutes alone.

Robin cleared the countertops and made Jeff a sandwich for his lunch. He must have become involved in his game with Cole's dog because he didn't rush in announcing he was hungry.

She went outside to stand on the small front porch and smiled as she watched Jeff and Blackie. Her son really had a way with animals—like his father. Every time Robin saw him play with Cole's Labrador, she marveled at how attuned to each other they were.

She smiled when she realized Cole was outside, too; he'd just finished watering his lawn.

"Jeff, I made a sandwich for you," she called.

"In a minute. Hey, Mom, watch," he yelled as he tossed a ball across the lawn. Blackie chased after it, skidding to a stop as he caught the bright red ball in his mouth.

"Come on, Blackie," Jeff urged. "Throw me the ball."

"He can't do that," Robin said in astonishment.

"Sure, he can. Just watch."

And just as Jeff had claimed, Blackie leapt into the air on all fours, tossed his head and sent the ball shooting into the street.

"I'll get it," Jeff hollered.

It was Cole's reaction that Robin noticed first. A horrified look came over his face and he threw down the hose. He was shouting even as he ran.

Like her son, Robin had been so caught up in Blackie's antics that she hadn't noticed the car barreling down the street, directly in Jeff's path.

CHAPTER EIGHT

"JEFF!" ROBIN SCREAMED, fear and panic choking her. Her hands flew to her mouth in relief as Cole grabbed Jeff around the waist and swept him out of the path of the speeding car. Together the two fell backward onto the wet grass. Robin raced over to them.

"Jeff, how many times have I told you to look before you run into the street? How many times?" Her voice was high and hysterical. "You deserve the spanking of your life for that stunt!"

"I saw the car," Jeff protested loudly. "I did! I was going to wait for it. Honest." He struggled to his feet, looking insulted at what he obviously considered an overreaction.

"Get into the house and wait for me there," Robin demanded, pointing furiously. She was trembling so badly she could barely speak.

Jeff brushed the grass from his jeans and lifted his head to a dignified angle, then casually walked toward the house. Not understanding, Blackie followed him, the rubber ball in his mouth, wanting to resume their play.

"I can't, boy," Jeff mumbled just loud enough for her to hear. "My mother just had some kind of anxiety attack that I'm gonna get punished for."

Cole's recovery was slower than Jeff's. He sat up and rubbed a hand across his eyes. His face was ashen, his expression stark with terror.

"Everything's all right. Jeff isn't hurt," Robin hurried to assure him. She slipped to her knees in front of him.

Cole nodded without looking at her. His eyes went blank and he slowly shook his head, as if to clear his mind.

"Cole," Robin said softly, "are you all right?"

"I . . . I don't know." He gave her a faint smile, but his eyes remained glazed and distant. He placed one hand over his heart and shook his head. "For a minute there I thought Jeff hadn't seen that car and . . . dear Lord, I don't know . . . if that boy had been hurt . . ."

"Thank you for acting so quickly," Robin whispered, gratitude and relief filling her heart. She ran her hands down the sides of his face, needing to touch him, seeking a way to comfort him, although her heart ached at his words. So many times over the past few weeks, she'd suspected—and feared—that Cole's feelings had more to do with replacing the family he'd lost than love for her and Jeff.

With a shudder, Cole locked his arms around her waist and pulled her close, burying his face in the gentle curve of her neck as he dragged deep gulps of air into his lungs.

"Come inside and I'll get us some coffee," Robin suggested.

Cole murmured agreement, but he didn't seem in any rush to release her. Nor she him. Her hands were in his hair and she rested her cheek against his, savoring these moments of closeness now that the panic was gone.

"I lost my son," Cole whispered and the words seemed to be wrenched from the deepest part of his soul. His voice held an agony only those who have suffered such a loss could understand. "In a car accident six years ago."

Robin kissed the crown of his head. "I know."

Cole broke away from her, slowly raising his eyes to meet hers. Mingled with profound grief was confusion. "Who told you?"

"Joyce Wallach."

Cole closed his eyes. "I could use that coffee."

They both stood, and when Cole wrapped his arm around her waist, Robin couldn't be sure it was to lend support or to offer it.

Inside the house, Jeff was sitting at the bottom of the stairs, his knees pressed under his chin. Ever loyal, Blackie lay beside him.

Jeff raised his head when Robin opened the front door, his round eyes following her. "I saw the car," he repeated. "You're getting upset over nothing. I hope you realize that. Hey, what's wrong with Cole?" he asked abruptly. He glanced from Robin to their neighbor and then back to his mother. "He looks like he's seen a ghost."

In some way, Robin supposed, Cole had.

"You all right, sport?" Cole asked. "I didn't hurt you when we fell, did I?"

"Naw." He bit his lip, eyes lowered.

Cole frowned. "You don't sound all that certain. Are you sure you're okay?"

Jeff nodded reluctantly. "I will be once I find out what my mother intends to do to me. I really was going to stop at the curb. Honest."

The kid would make an excellent attorney, Robin decided.

"I think I might have overreacted," Cole said. He held open his arms and Jeff flew into them without a second's hesitation. Briefly Cole's eyes drifted shut, as though in silent thanksgiving for Jeff's safety.

"I didn't mean to frighten you," Jeff murmured. "I would have stopped."

"I know."

"I promise to be more careful."

"I certainly hope so," Robin said.

Cole released Jeff and sighed deeply, then looked at Robin. "You said something about coffee?"

She smiled and nodded. "I'll get it in a minute. All right, Jeff, you can go outside, but from now on if you're playing ball with Blackie, do it in the backyard. Understand?"

"Sure, Mom," her son said eagerly. "But—" he paused "—you mean that's it? You aren't going to ground me or anything? I mean, of course you aren't going to because I did everything I was supposed to—well, almost everything. Thanks, Mom." He tossed the red ball into the air and deftly caught it with one hand. "Come on, Blackie, we just got a pardon from the governor."

Robin followed the pair into the kitchen and watched as Jeff opened the sliding glass door and raced into the backyard with Blackie in hot pursuit. Reassured, she poured them each a mug of coffee while Cole pulled out one of the kitchen chairs. She carried the mugs to the table, then sat down across from him.

Cole immediately reached for her hand, lacing her fingers with his own. He focused his concentration on their linked hands. "Bobby was my son. He died when he was ten."

"Jeff's age," Robin said as a chill surrounded her heart.

"Bobby was so full of laughter and life I couldn't be around him and not smile."

Talking about Bobby was clearly difficult for Cole, and Robin longed to do or say something that would help. But she could think of nothing to ease the agony etched so deeply on his handsome face.

"He was the kind of boy every father dreams of having. Inquisitive, sensitive, full of mischief. Gifted with a vivid imagination."

"A lot like Jeff," she murmured, and her hands tightened around the mug.

Cole nodded. "Bobby used to tell me that I shouldn't worry about Janice—she was my wife—because *he*, my ten-year-old son, was taking care of her."

Robin held her breath as she watched the fierce pain in his eyes. "You don't need to tell me this." Not if it was going to rip open wounds that weren't properly healed yet.

"I should have told you long before this," he said, frowning slightly. "It's just that even now, after all these years, it's still difficult to talk about my son. For a good many years, I felt as though a part of me had died with Bobby. The very best part of me. I don't believe that anymore."

"Jeff reminds you a lot of Bobby, doesn't he?" Robin doubted Cole fully understood that he was transferring his love from one boy to the other.

A reluctant smile tugged at the corners of his mouth. "Bobby had a huskier build and was taller than Jeff. His sport was basketball, but he was more of a spectator than a participant. His real love was computers. Had he lived, I think Bobby would have gone into that field. Janice never understood that. She wanted him to be more athletic, and he tried to please her." Cole's gaze dropped to his hands. "Janice and I were divorced before the accident happened. She died with him. If there's anything to be grateful for in their deaths, it's the knowledge that they both went instantly. I couldn't have stood knowing that they'd suffered." He paused long enough to take a sip of the coffee, and grimaced once. "You added sugar?"

"I thought you might need it."

He chuckled. "I have so much to thank you for."

"Me?"

"Do you remember the afternoon Jeff ran away?"

She wasn't likely to forget it. With Jeff around, Robin always figured she didn't need to do aerobic exercise to keep her heart in shape. Her son managed to do it with his antics.

"I left on a business trip to Seattle soon afterward," he reminded her.

"I remember." That was when Jeff had watched Blackie for him.

"Late one afternoon, when the meeting was over and dinner wasn't scheduled for another couple of hours, I went for a stroll," Cole said. "It was still light and I found myself on the waterfront. The sky was a vivid blue and the waters green and clear. It's funny I would remember that, but it's all so distinct in my memory. I stood alone on the pier and watched as a ferry headed for one of the islands, cutting a path through the waves. Something brought Bobby to my mind, although he's never far from my thoughts, even now. The most amazing thing happened that afternoon. It's difficult to find the words to explain." He hesitated, as though searching for a way to make Robin understand. Then apparently he gave up the effort and slowly shook his head.

"Tell me about it," Robin suggested in a quiet voice.

"Well, standing there at the end of the pier...I don't know. For the first time since I lost my son, I felt his presence more than I did his absence. It was as if he was there at my side, pointing out the Olympic Mountains to me and asking questions. Bobby was always full of questions. My heart felt lighter than it had in years—as though the heavy burden of pain and grief had been lifted from my shoulders. For no reason whatsoever, I started to smile. I think I've been smiling ever since. And laughing. And feeling.

"When I got back to the hotel, I had the sudden urge to hear your voice. I didn't have any excuse to call you, so I phoned on the pretense of talking to Jeff and checking up on Blackie. But it was your voice I wanted to hear."

Robin smiled through the unexpected rush of tears that clouded her eyes, wondering if Cole realized what he was saying. It might have been her voice he thought he wanted to hear, but it was Jeff he'd called.

"I found a new freedom on that Seattle pier. It was as if, in that moment, I was released from the past. I can't say exactly what it was that changed. Meeting you and Jeff played a big role in it, I recognize that much, but it was more than that. It was as if something deep inside me was willing to admit that it was finally time to let go."

"I'm glad for you," Robin whispered, not knowing what else to say.

"The problem is, I never allowed myself to properly grieve or deal with the anger I felt toward Janice. She was driving at the time and the accident was her fault. Yet deep in my heart I know she would never purposely have done anything to injure Bobby. She loved him as much as I did. He was her son, too.

"It wasn't until I met you that I realized I had to forgive Janice. I was never the kind of husband she needed and I'm afraid I was a disappointment to her. Only in the last couple of years of our marriage was I willing to accept that she suffered from a serious emotional and mental illness. Her addiction to alcohol was as much a disease as cancer. I didn't understand or accept her weakness, and because of that we all suffered."

"You're being too hard on yourself," Robin said, but she doubted Cole even heard her.

"The anger and the grief were a constant gnawing pain. I refused to acknowledge or deal with either emotion. Over the years, instead of healing, the agony of my loss grew more intense. I closed myself off from friends and colleagues and threw myself into my work, spending far more time in the office than I did at home. Blackie was virtually my only companion. And then a few years ago I started working on my place in the country. But the pleasure that gave me came from hard physical work, the kind that leaves you too tired to think." His features softened and he smiled at her. "I'd forgotten what it was to fly a kite or laze in the sunshine."

"That was why you suggested the picnic with Jeff and me?"

He grinned and his dark eyes seemed almost boyish. "The last time I was in Golden Gate Park was with Bobby, shortly before the accident. Deciding to have a picnic there was a giant step for me. I half expected to feel some pangs of grief, if not a full-blown assault. Instead I experienced a joy and appreciation for the renewal I felt. Laughter is a gift I'd forgotten. You and Jeff helped me realize that, as well."

Everything Cole was saying confirmed her worst fears.

"Mom!" Jeff roared into the kitchen with Blackie at his heels. "Is there anything decent to eat around here? Are you guys still going out to dinner? I don't suppose you'd consider bringing me, would you?"

Cole chuckled, then leapt to his feet to playfully muss Jeff's hair. "Not this time, sport. Tonight is for your mother and me."

TWO HOURS LATER, as Robin stood in front of the bathroom mirror, she had her doubts about agreeing to this dinner date. She was falling in love with a man who hadn't fully dealt with the pain of losing his son and his wife. Perhaps she recognized it in Cole because she saw the same things in herself. She loved Lonny and always would. He'd died years earlier and she still found herself talking to him, refusing to involve herself in another relationship. A part of her continued to grieve and seemed it always would.

Examining herself in the mirror, Robin surveyed her calf-length skirt of soft blue velvet, and white silk blouse with a large teardrop pearl pin tucked at the neck.

She was fussing with her hair, pinning one side back with combs and studying the effect, when Jeff strolled into her room. He leaned casually against the doorway, a bag of potato chips in his hand.

"Hey, you look nice."

"Don't sound so surprised." She decided she'd spent enough time on her hair and fastened her pearl earrings. Jeff was disappointed about not joining them, but he'd been a good sport—especially after Cole promised him lunch at a special fish-and-chip place on the Wharf the following Saturday.

"You're wearing your pearls?" Jeff mumbled, mouth full of potato chips.

"Yes," Robin said, turning to face him. "Do they look all right?"

Jeff's halfhearted shrug didn't do a lot to boost Robin's confidence. "I suppose. I don't know about stuff like that. Mrs. Lawrence could probably tell you." He popped another potato chip into his mouth and munched loudly. "My dad gave you those earrings, didn't he?"

"For our first wedding anniversary."

Jeff nodded. "I thought so." His look grew reflective. "When I grow up and get married, will I do mushy stuff like that?"

"Like what?"

"Waste a bunch of money on something that dangles from a woman's ear?"

"Probably," Robin said, not bothering to disguise her amusement. "And lots of other things, too. Like taking your wife to dinner and telling her how beautiful she is and how much you love her."

"Yuck!" Jeff wrinkled his nose. "You really know how to ruin a guy's appetite." With that he turned to march down the stairs, taking his potato chips with him.

Robin stood at the top of the staircase. "Cole will be here any minute, so you can go over to Kelly's now," she called down.

"All right. I put my plate in the dishwasher. Is there anything you want me to tell Kelly's mom?"

"Just that I won't be too late."

"You're sure I can't come with you?" Jeff tried one more time.

Robin didn't give him an answer, knowing he didn't honestly expect one. After a moment, Jeff grumbled for show, then headed out the front door for the neighbor's.

Robin returned to the bathroom and smiled into the mirror, picturing Jeff several years into the future and seeing Lonny's handsome face smiling back at her. She was warmed by the image, certain that her son would grow into as fine a young man as his father had been. Robin couldn't ask for anything more.

"You don't mind that I'm wearing the pearls for Cole, do you?" she asked her dead husband, although she knew he would never have objected. She ran the tips of her fingers over them, feeling reassured.

The doorbell chimed just as Robin dabbed perfume to the pulse points at her neck and wrists. She drew in a calming breath, glanced quickly at her reflection once again, then walked down the stairs to answer the door.

Cole was dressed in a black pin-striped suit and looked so handsome that her breath caught. He smiled as she let him in, but for the life of her, she couldn't think of a solitary thing to say.

His eyes held hers as he reached for her hands. Slowly, he lowered his gaze, taking in the way she'd styled her hair, the pearl pin and the outfit she'd chosen with such care.

"You are so beautiful," he said.

"I was just thinking the same about you," she confessed.

His mouth tilted in a grin. "If I kiss you, will it ruin your lipstick?"

"Probably."

"I'm going to kiss you, anyway," he said in a husky murmur that tugged at her heart. Tenderly he fit his mouth to hers, weaving his fingers through her hair. The kiss was gentle and slow and thorough. A single kiss, and she was clay ready to be molded. The realization struck her hard. When Cole touched her, Robin felt alive all the way to the soles of her feet. *Alive.* Healthy. A red-blooded woman. When he released her, she was shocked to find that she was trembling. From the inside out.

"I've mussed your hair," he apologized. His hands found her nape under the soft cloud of hair.

"And you've got lipstick on your mouth," she managed quaveringly, reaching up to wipe it away with her fingers. "There. It'll only take me a moment to fix my hair," she said, picking up her purse and moving to the hallway mirror.

He stood behind her, his hands on her shoulders as she brushed her hair, then carefully tucked the loose curls back into place with the tortoiseshell combs.

"Are you ready?" he asked when she'd finished.

Robin nodded, unable to find her voice.

Cole led her outside to his car and held open the passenger door. He glanced around, then dropped a quick kiss on her unsuspecting lips. He chuckled at her look of surprise as he hurried around the car, his movements lighthearted, and slipped into the driver's seat.

"You didn't tell me where we're having dinner."

"I told Heather Lawrence in case she needs to get hold of you for anything, but otherwise, it's a surprise."

Robin wasn't sure what to think. A number of San Francisco's restaurants were famous internationally, but her knowledge of fancy dining places was limited. She assumed this one was somewhere in the heart of the city, until he exited from the freeway heading south along Highway 101 toward the ocean.

"Cole?" she asked hesitantly.

"Don't worry," he said, casting her a swift glance that didn't conceal the mischievous twinkle in his eyes. "I promise you dinner will be worth the drive."

The restaurant sat high on a cliff, with a stunning view of the surf battering against jagged rocks below.

Cole parked the Porsche, then came around to help her out, taking the opportunity to steal another kiss. It was with obvious reluctance that he released her. His arm found her waist as he directed her toward the doors leading into the elegant restaurant. The maître d' escorted them to a table that overlooked the water and with a flourish presented them with elaborate menus.

Robin scanned the list of entrées, impressed with the interesting variations on basic themes. She was less impressed with the prices—a single dinner cost as much as an entire week's worth of lunches. For her *and* Jeff.

"When you said fancy you weren't joking, were you?" she whispered, biting her lip.

Cole lowered his menu and sent her a vibrant smile. "Tonight is special," he said simply.

"You're telling me. If I wasn't having dinner with you, I'd probably have eaten a toasted cheese sandwich and a bowl of tomato soup with Jeff."

Their waiter appeared and both ordered one of the restaurant's specialties—a scallop and shrimp sauté—which proved as succulent and spicy as the menu had promised.

They talked through dinner and afterward, over steaming cups of Irish coffee. It amazed Robin that they had so much to say to one another, although they hadn't touched on the issue closest to her heart. But she hesitated to broach the subject of Cole's relationship with Jeff. She didn't want to risk the delightful camaraderie they were sharing tonight. Their conversation could have gone on for hours and in fact did. They talked about the books they'd read, recent movies they'd seen, records they liked. It came as a pleasant surprise to discover that their tastes in music were similar. And they preferred many of the same authors.

All evening they laughed, they argued, they talked, as if they'd been friends most of their lives. Cole grinned so often, it was hard for Robin to remember that she'd once actually wondered if the man ever smiled.

Robin told Cole about her job and how much she enjoyed accounting. She voiced her fears about not being the kind of mother she wanted to be for Jeff. "There are so many things I want to share with Jeff that I don't have time for. There just aren't enough hours in a day."

Cole talked about his career goals and his dreams. He spoke of the forty acres willed to him by his grandfather and how he'd once longed to close himself off from the world by moving there.

"But you aren't going to now?" Robin asked.

"No. I no longer have any reason to hide. The house is nearly finished and I may still move there, but I'll maintain my work schedule." He stared down into his steaming coffee. "I was approached last week about running for the state senate."

Robin's heart swelled with pride. "Are you going to do it?"

"No. I'm not the right man for politics. I'll support someone else, but a political career doesn't interest me. It never has, although I admit to being flattered."

A band started playing then, and several couples took to the dance floor.

"Shall we?" Cole asked, nodding in that direction.

"Oh, Cole, I don't know. The last time I danced was at my cousin's wedding ten years ago. I'm afraid I'll step all over your feet."

"I'm game if you are."

She was reluctant but agreed to try. They stood, and she moved naturally into his embrace, as if they'd been partners for years. Robin's eyes slowly closed when Cole folded her in his arms, tucking her head against the side of his chin. In that moment she experienced a surge of joy that surprised her with its intensity.

The dance ended, but they didn't leave the floor.

"Have I told you how lovely you are?" Cole asked, his mouth close to her ear.

Robin grinned and nodded. "Twice. Once when you picked me up at the house and once during the meal. I know you're exaggerating, but ..." She hesitated, then added, "When I'm with you, I feel beautiful."

"I don't think a woman's ever paid me a higher compliment."

She raised her eyes and was shocked by the powerful emotions in his.

"Do you mind if we leave now?" he surprised her by asking.

"No, of course not, if that's what you want."

He frowned. "If it were up to me I'd spend the rest of the night right here with you in my arms, but I have this sudden need to kiss you, and if I do it here and do it properly, we're going to attract a lot of attention."

Cole quickly paid the bill and he hurried Robin to the car. The minute they were settled inside, he reached for her. He did as he'd promised, kissing her until she was breathless and weak. Her arms clung to him and his mouth sought hers once more.

"At least I'm not making you cry this time," he said softly.

"That still embarrasses me," she admitted. "It's never happened with anyone. Ever. I still don't understand it. I don't know if I ever will."

"I don't think I'll ever forget it."

"Please do."

"No," he said, shaking his head. "It touched me in a way I can't explain. It helped me realize that I was going to love you. After Janice and Bobby, I doubted there was any love left in me to give. You taught me otherwise. Jeff taught me otherwise. My heart is full and has been almost from the moment we met." He took her hand and pressed her palm to his heart. "Do you feel it?"

Robin nodded. "It's beating so hard," she whispered.

"That's because I'm nervous."

"Nervous? About what?"

Cole slid a hand into his pocket and brought out a small black velvet box.

Robin's heart started to pound in double time. "Cole?" she said anxiously, not sure what she should think or how she should act.

"I love you, Robin." His voice was hoarse. "I realized it the moment I heard your voice when I called from Seattle. And every moment since has convinced me how right it is to love you." He opened the box and revealed the largest diamond Robin had ever seen. Slowly he raised his eyes to hers. "I'm asking you to be my wife."

CHAPTER NINE

"YOU MEAN THIS WHOLE evening...you arranged this because you intended to ask me to marry you?" Robin asked, pressing the tips of her fingers to her trembling lips. Despite her fears a gentle gladness suffused in her heart.

"Surely it isn't that much of a surprise?" he murmured. "I've never made an effort to hide the way I feel about you or how much I enjoy Jeff."

Contrary to what Cole might think, his proposal *did* come as a surprise. "I . . . I don't know what to say."

"A simple yes would suit me," Cole urged warmly.

"But... Oh, Cole, it would be so easy to marry you, so easy to link my life and Jeff's to yours and never look back, but I don't know if it would be right for us or for you. There's so much to consider, so many factors to weigh in a decision this important. I'd like nothing better than to say yes, but I just can't do it."

"Are you asking for time?" Cole's eyes seemed to penetrate hers, even in the dark.

"Please." For now, that seemed the simplest thing to say, although her hesitation was based on something much deeper. Cole had found a peace within himself since meeting her and Jeff; he'd told her so that very afternoon. She was tempted to say yes, to turn away from her doubts and agree to marry him. Cole had been so good for Jeff, so wonderful to her.

"I hate to disappoint you," she murmured, sadness weighing down her voice.

"I know exactly what you're thinking, exactly how you're feeling."

"You do?" Somehow she doubted it. But knowing she couldn't delay it any longer, she jumped in with both feet. "I was...just thinking about what you told me this afternoon. How you'd recently dealt with the loss of Janice and Bobby. While you were talking, I couldn't help feeling your exhilaration. You've obviously found a newborn sense of freedom. I think the question you need to ask yourself is if this rebirth you've experienced is what prompted the idea of marrying again."

"No," he said flatly. "Falling in love with you did."

"Oh, Cole," she whispered. "It must seem like fate to have Jeff and me move in next door, and it gets more complicated with Jeff being the same age as Bobby...."

"Maybe it does all appear too convenient, but if I was just looking for a woman and a child, then Heather Lawrence would have filled the bill. It's you I fell in love with."

"But how can you be so sure?" she countered quickly. "We barely know each other."

Cole smiled at her doubts. "The first time we kissed was enough to convince me I was going to love you. It was the Friday night after I returned from Seattle, remember?"

Robin nodded, wincing a little.

"I was so stunned by the powerful effect that kiss had on me that I avoided you for an entire week afterward. If you want the truth, I was terrified. You'll have to remember, up until that time I was convinced

I was incapable of ever falling in love again. One kiss and I felt jolted to the core. You hit me hard, Robin, right between the eyes, and I needed time to step back and analyze what was happening. That's the reason I don't have any qualms now about giving you however long you need to sort out what you're feeling. I want you to be very sure.''

Robin released a pent-up sigh and her shoulders heaved. Cole folded her in his arms and his chin brushed against the crown of her head while his hands roved in wide circles across her back. The action was soothing and gentle. She was beginning to feel more confident in his love, but she had to be careful. She *wanted* him to love her, because she was so much in love with him.

Cole tucked a finger under her chin and lifted her face to his. As their eyes met, he slanted his mouth over hers in a wildly possessive kiss, a kiss filled with undisguised need.

When he broke away, Robin was trembling. She buried her face in his neck and drew several deep breaths.

"If you're going to take some time to think about things," Cole whispered against her hair, "then I wanted to give you something more to think about."

"HAVE YOU HAD A CHANCE to check those figures on—" Angela began, then stopped abruptly, waving her hand in front of Robin's face.

"A chance to check what figures?" Robin asked, making a determined effort to focus. She knew she'd been behaving like a sleepwalker most of the morning, but she couldn't stop thinking about Cole's marriage proposal.

"What's with you today?" Angela demanded. "Every time I look over here, I find you staring into space with this perplexed expression on your face."

"I was ... just thinking," Robin muttered.

"About what?"

"Nothing," Robin insisted.

"Come on, girl, you know better than that. You can't fool me." Angela leaned her hip against the edge of Robin's desk and crossed her arms, taking her usual aggressive stance. "I've known you far too long, and from everything you *haven't* said, I'd guess your handsome neighbor's involved. What's he done now?"

"Cole? What makes you ask anything so ridiculous?"

Angela frowned, shaking her head slowly. Then she stretched out her hands and made a come-hither motion. "Tell Mama everything," she intoned. "You might as well get it over with and tell me now, because you know that sooner or later I'm going to drag it out of you. I always do. What kind of friend would I be if I didn't extract your deepest darkest secrets?"

"He took me to dinner," Robin admitted, knowing that Angela was right. Sooner or later, she'd wheedle it out of her.

"Where'd he take you?"

She shrugged, wanting to keep that to herself. "It was outside the city."

"*Where* outside the city?" Angela pressed.

"Heavens, I don't know. Somewhere along the coast on Highway 101."

Angela uncrossed her arms and started pacing in front of Robin's desk. "It wasn't the Cliffhouse, was it?"

"I . . . I think it might have been," Robin murmured, concentrating on the task in front of her. The one she should have finished several hours earlier, but hadn't. The one she couldn't seem to focus on, even now.

"Aha!" Angela cried, pointing her index finger toward the ceiling, like the detective in a comic spoof.

"What?" Robin cried.

"If Cole took you to the Cliffhouse, he did it for a reason."

"Of course he did. The food was fabulous. By the way, you were right about Frank, he's exceptionally nice," Robin said hurriedly, in an effort to interrupt her friend's line of thought before she inadvertently stumbled on the reason for Robin's pensive mood.

"You already told me what you think of Frank, remember?" Angela muttered, tapping her finger against her lips. "Cole took you to dinner at the Cliffhouse," she repeated slowly, as though reviewing a vital clue in a puzzling murder mystery.

"To be honest, I think his choice of restaurant had something to do with Frank," Robin inserted, tossing her sleuth friend a red herring.

"So Cole was jealous?"

"Not exactly," Robin said, leaning back in her chair. "Well, maybe a little," she amended, knowing Angela would never believe her if she denied it completely. "I mean, Cole did invite me to dinner as soon as he learned I was dining with Frank, so I guess you could say he was a little jealous. But not much. Cole's not the jealous type—he told me that himself."

"I see." Angela was frowning as she walked back to her desk. Her look remained thoughtful for the rest of the morning, though she didn't question Robin again.

But when they left for lunch, she showed a renewed interest in the subject of Cole.

"How's Jeff?" she began as they stood in line in the employees' cafeteria.

"Fine," Robin said as she reached for a plastic tray.

"That's all you're going to say?"

"What more do you want to know?"

"I ask about Jeff once a week or so, then sit back and listen for the next fifteen minutes while you tell me about the latest craziness he's led you into," Angela said heatedly. "It never fails. You've told me about him running away with a frying pan and an atlas. You've bragged about what a fabulous pitcher he's turning out to be, and you list a multitude of details about every game he's played. After you tell me all about his athletic ability, you generally mention how good he is with animals and all the tricks he's taught Blackie in the past week or so.

"Today I innocently ask how Jeff is, and what do I get? *Fine*. All right, Robin, tell me what happened with Cole Camden before I go loony trying to figure it out."

"It's something I need to figure out myself," Robin insisted. She paused to study the salads before selecting a mound of cottage cheese and setting it on her tray.

"What are you doing now?" Angela cried, throwing her arms in the air. "You hate cottage cheese. You never eat it unless you're upset about something and looking for ways to punish yourself." She lifted the small bowl from Robin's tray and replaced it with a fresh fruit salad, shaking her head the entire time.

The problem with Angela was that she knew Robin all too well.

They progressed a little farther down the line. Robin stood in front of the entrées, but before she chose one, she glanced at her friend. "You want to pick one out for me here, too?" she asked dryly.

"Yes, I do, before you end up requesting liver and onions."

Angela picked the lasagna, thick with melted cheese and spicy Italian sauce. "If you're looking for ways to punish yourself, girl, there are tastier methods."

Despite her thoughtful mood, Robin found herself smiling.

Once they'd paid for their lunches, Angela led her to a window table that offered a certain amount of privacy. Robin busied herself arranging her dishes on the table and set the tray aside.

Angela sat directly across from her, elbows braced on either side of her lunch. "Are you sure there isn't anything more you'd care to tell me?"

"About what?"

"About you and Cole. I can't remember the last time I saw you like this. It's as if you're trapped in some kind of maze and can't find your way out."

The description was so apt that Robin felt a tingling sensation along her spine. She did feel hopelessly lost. Her mind was cluttered, her emotions confused. She had one foot in the present, one foot in the past, and didn't know which way to turn.

"I talked to Frank on Sunday afternoon," Angela continued, dipping her fork into a crisp green salad. "He said he enjoyed the evening you spent with him, too, but doubted you'd be seeing each other again because it was obvious to him you were in love with Cole Camden. In fact, Frank said you talked about little else the entire evening."

"He said all that, did he?"

Angela nodded. "He's right, isn't he? You are in love with Cole, aren't you?"

"I . . . I don't know."

"What do you mean you don't know?" Angela persisted. "It's written all over you. You've got that glazed look and you walk around in a trance, practically bumping into walls."

"You make it sound like I need an ambulance."

"Or a doctor," Angela whispered, leaning across the table as far as possible. "Or maybe a lawyer . . . That's it!" she said loud enough to attract the attention of several people at nearby tables. "Cole took you to bed, and now you're so confused you don't know what to do. I told you I'd stumble on the answer sooner or later." Her eyes flashed triumphantly.

"That's not it," Robin declared, half rising from the table in hot denial. She could feel the color crowding into her cheeks as she glanced around the cafeteria. When she sat back down, she covered her face with both hands. "If you must know, Cole asked me to marry him."

A moment of shocked silence followed before Angela shrieked with pure delight. "That's fabulous! Wonderful! Good grief, woman, what's wrong with you? You should be in seventh heaven. It isn't every day a handsome, wealthy, wonderful man extends a proposal of marriage. I hope to high heaven you leapt at the chance." She hesitated, growing suddenly still. "Robin? You did tell him you'd marry him, didn't you?"

Robin swallowed and slowly shook her head. "No. I asked him for some time to think things through."

"Think things through?" Angela squealed. "What is there to think through? He's rich. He's handsome. He's in love with you and crazy about Jeff. What more could you possibly want from the man?"

Tears brimmed in Robin's eyes as she looked up to meet her friend's avid gaze. "I think he's more in love with the idea of having a family than he's interested in me."

"IS COLE COMING?" Jeff asked, working the stiffness out of his baseball mitt by slamming his fist into the middle of it several times.

"I don't know," Robin said, glancing toward their neighbor's house as they walked to the car. "I haven't talked to him in the last few days."

"I noticed. You're not mad at him, are you?"

"Of course not," Robin said, sliding into the driver's seat of her compact. "We've both been busy."

Jeff fingered the bill of his baseball cap, then secured the cap to his head. "I saw him yesterday and told him about the game, and he said he might come. I hope he does."

Secretly Robin hoped Cole would be there, too. Over the past five days, she'd discovered she missed not talking to him. She hadn't come to any decision, but he hadn't pressed her to make one, willing to offer her all the time she needed. Robin hadn't realized how accustomed she'd grown to his presence. How much she needed to see him and talk to him. Exchange smiles and glances. Touch him...

When she was married to Lonny, they were two people very much in love, two people who'd linked their lives to form one whole. But Lonny had been taken from her, and for a long time afterward, Robin had stumbled through life with a huge part of her missing.

All week she'd swayed back and forth over Cole's proposal, wondering if she should ignore her doubts. Wondering if she *could* ignore them. Sleepless nights hadn't yielded the answer. Neither had long solitary walks in Balboa Park while Jeff practiced with his baseball team.

"Cole said—" Jeff started to say, then stopped abruptly as his hands flew to his head. A panicky look broke out on his face and he stared at Robin.

"What's wrong? Did you forget something?"

"My lucky hat!" Jeff cried. "It's on my dresser. We have to go back."

"For a baseball cap?" Robin didn't bother to disguise how silly she considered that idea. "You're wearing a baseball cap. What's wrong with that one?"

"It won't work. You have to understand, Mom, it's my *lucky* hat. Not an ordinary one. I've been wearing it every since we played our first game. I had that very same hat when I hit my first two home runs. I can't play without it," he explained frantically. "We have to go back. Hurry, or we'll be late for the game. Turn here," he cried, pointing at the closest intersection.

"Jeff," she said, hoping to reason with her son. "It isn't the hat that makes you play well."

"I knew you were going to say something like that," he muttered, "and deep down I know it's probably true, but I want to be on the safe side, just in case. We've got to go back and get that hat!"

Knowing it would only waste valuable time and effort to argue, Robin did as he requested. After all, his entire career as a major-league pitcher hung in the balance!

She was smiling as she entered her driveway. Sitting in the car while Jeff ran inside for his lucky cap, Robin glanced over at Cole's place. His car was gone. It had been since early that morning, and she suspected he was at the property, working on his house. Jeff would be disappointed about Cole missing his game, but he'd understand.

Jeff came barreling out of the house, slamming the front door. He leapt into the car and fastened his seat belt. "Come on, Mom," he said anxiously, "let's get this show on the road." As if she'd caused the delay, Robin thought to herself, amused by her son's sudden impatience.

By the time they arrived at Balboa Park, the lot was filled to overflowing. Robin was fortunate enough to find a space on the street, a minor miracle in itself. Perhaps there was something to this magic-cap business after all.

Jeff ran across the grass, hurrying toward his teammates, leaving Robin to fend for herself, which was fine. He had his precious cap and was content.

The bleachers were crowded with parents. Robin found a seat close to the top and had just settled into place when she saw Cole making his way toward her. Her heart did an immediate flip-flop before righting itself. It wasn't until he sat next to her that she found her tongue.

"I thought you were working up on the property this weekend."

"And miss seeing Jeff pitch? Wild horses couldn't have kept me away." He was smiling at her with that cocky heart-stopping smile of his.

"How have you been?" she asked, unable to keep her eyes off him. He looked too good to be true, and his dark gaze was filled with warmth and tenderness. How could she help getting lost in eyes that generous? It seemed impossible to fight him any longer.

"I've missed you like crazy," he whispered, and the humor seemed to drain out of him as his eyes searched hers. "I didn't think it was possible to feel this alone. Not anymore."

"I've missed you, too."

He seemed to relax once she'd said that. "Thank you," he said quietly. "Have you been thinking about what I said last weekend?"

She lowered her head. "I haven't thought of anything else."

"Then you've made up your mind?"

"No." She kept her face lowered, not wanting him to read her confusion.

He tilted her chin with one finger, forcing her to meet his eyes. "I promised myself I wouldn't ask you and then I couldn't seem to stop myself. I won't again."

She offered him a weak smile, and Cole looked around him, clearly wanting to kiss her, but not in front of such a large gathering. The funny part was, Robin didn't care about being seen. She was so hungry for the reassurance of his touch, it didn't matter to her that they were in the middle of a crowded park.

"I see Jeff's wearing his lucky hat," Cole said, clasping her hand and giving her fingers a comforting squeeze.

"You know all about that?"

"Of course. Jeff tells me everything."

"He panicked when he realized he was wearing the wrong one, and I had to make a U-turn in the middle

of the street because he'd left the guaranteed-to-pitch-
well baseball cap on his dresser.''

"You can't blame him. The luck has lasted through
five games now.''

"I wonder if it'll last until he reaches the pros,''
Robin said, sharing a smile with him.

"You're doing all right?'' Cole asked unexpectedly.

She nodded, although it wasn't entirely true. Now
that she was with Cole, every doubt she'd struggled
with all week vanished like fog under an afternoon
sun. Only when they were apart was she forced to
confront her fears.

"After Jeff's finished here, let's do something together,'' Cole suggested. "The three of us.''

She nodded, unable to refuse him anything.

"Come to think of it, didn't I promise Jeff lunch?
I seem to recall making a rash pledge to buy him fish-
and-chips because we were leaving him with Heather
and Kelly Lawrence when we went to dinner last
week.''

Robin grinned. "It seems to me he said something
about that.''

They went to a cheerful little fish-and-chip restaurant down by the Wharf. The weather had been chilly
all morning, but the sun was out in full force by early
afternoon. Jeff was excited about his team's latest win
and attributed it all to the luck brought to them by his
cap.

After a leisurely lunch, the three of them strolled
along the busy waterfront. Robin bought a loaf of
fresh sourdough bread and a small bouquet of spring
flowers. Jeff found a plastic snake he couldn't bear to
live without and paid for it with his allowance.

"Just wait till Jimmy Wallach sees this!'' he crowed.

"I'm more curious to see how Kelly Lawrence reacts," Robin said.

"Oh, Kelly likes snakes," Jeff told them cheerfully. "Jimmy was over one day and I thought I'd scare Kelly with a live garden snake, but it was Jimmy who started screaming. Kelly said snakes were just one of God's creatures and there was nothing to be afraid of. Isn't it just like a girl to get religious about a snake?"

Jeff raced down the sidewalk while Cole and Robin stood at the end of the pier.

"You look tired," Cole said, as his fingers gently touched her forehead, brushing back the thick curls.

"I'm fine," she insisted, gazing out at the cool green waters of San Francisco Bay. But Cole was right; she hadn't been sleeping well.

"I see so much of myself in you," Cole said softly. His words surprised her. "How's that?"

"The pain mostly. How many years has Lonny been dead?"

"Ten. In some ways I'm still grieving for him." She couldn't be less than honest with Cole.

"You're not sure if you can love another man, are you? At least not with the same intensity that you loved Jeff's father."

"That's not it at all. I . . . I just don't know if I can stop loving him."

Cole went very still. "I never intended to take Lonny away from you or Jeff. He's a part of your past, an important part. Being married to Lonny, giving birth to Jeff, contributed to making you what you are." He paused, and they both remained silent.

"Bobby had been buried for six years before I had the courage to face the future. I hung on to my grief, carried it with me everywhere I went, dragging it like a heavy piece of luggage I couldn't travel without."

"I'm not that way about Lonny," she countered, ready to argue, not heatedly or vehemently, but logically, because what he was saying simply wasn't true. She grieved for her dead husband, felt his absence, but she hadn't allowed this sense of loss to destroy her life.

"Perhaps you aren't grieving as intensely as you once were," Cole amended. "But I wonder, really wonder, if you honestly have laid your husband to rest."

"Of course I have," she answered with a gentle nod of her head, not wanting to talk about Lonny.

"I don't mean to sound unsympathetic," Cole said, his tone compassionate. "I understand, believe me I do. Emotional pain is familiar territory for us both. It seems to me that sustaining this kind of grief is like pitching a tent in the barren soil and lingering there, afraid of what lies just beyond."

"You're exaggerating, Cole."

"Maybe," he agreed. "You're a lovely woman, Robin. Witty. Intelligent. Outgoing. I'm sure one of the first questions anyone asks you is how long it's been since your husband died. And I'll bet when you tell them, they seem surprised."

That was true, and Robin wondered how Cole had guessed.

"Most young widows remarry."

"Are you suggesting that because I didn't immediately find my way back into matrimonial bliss I'm a candidate for therapy? Come on, Cole, even you must realize how ridiculous that is."

"Even me?" he asked, chuckling.

Jeff came racing toward them, his face flushed with excitement. "They're filming a movie," he cried, pointing toward a congested area farther down the pier. "There's cameras and actors and everything. Can I go watch some more?"

Robin nodded. "Just don't get in anyone's way. Understand?"

Jeff nodded. "I won't. Promise. Here, Mom, hold my snake." He entrusted her with his precious package before racing back down the pier.

"He's a fine boy, Robin."

"He loves you already. You and Blackie."

"And what about his mother?"

The knot in her throat thickened. "She loves you, too."

Cole grinned. "She just isn't sure if she can let go of her dead husband to take on a live one. Am I right?"

His words hit their mark. "I don't know," she admitted finally. "Maybe it's because I'm so afraid you want to marry me because Jeff reminds you of Bobby. Or because you've created a fantasy wife and think I'll fit the role."

Her words seemed to shock him. "No. You've got that all wrong. Jeff is a wonderful plus in this relationship, but it's *you* I fell in love with. It's you I want to grow old with. You, and you alone, not some ideal. If you want to know the truth, I think you're stirring up all this turmoil because you're afraid of ever marrying again. The little world you've made is tidy and safe. But is this what Lonny would have wanted for you?" He gripped her firmly by the shoulders. "If Lonny were standing beside you right now, and you could ask him about marrying me, what would he say?"

"I don't understand."

"If you could seek Lonny's advice, what would he tell you? Would he say, 'Robin, look at this guy. He's in love with you. He thinks the world of Jeff, and he's ready to embark on a new life. This is an opportunity too good for you to pass up. Don't be a fool. Marry him.'?"

"That sounds like something my friend Angela would say."

"I think I'm going to like this friend of yours just as long as she doesn't try to set you up with another one of her divorced cousins," Cole said, laughing. His eyes grew warm as he gazed at her, and she suspected he was longing to take her in his arms and kiss her doubts away. But he didn't. Instead, he looked over his shoulder and sighed. "I think I'll go check and see what Jeff's up to. I'll leave you to yourself for a few minutes. I don't mean to pressure you, but I do want you to think about what I said."

"You aren't pressuring me," she whispered, staring out over the water.

Cole left her then, and her hands gripped the steel railing as she raised her eyes to the sky. "Oh, Lonny," she whispered. "What should I do?"

CHAPTER TEN

"COLE WANTS ME to ask your advice." Robin continued to look up at the cloudless blue sky. "Oh, Lonny, I honestly don't know what's right for Jeff and me anymore. I love Cole. I love you. But at the same time I can't help wondering about Cole's motives...."

Robin paused, waiting. Not that she expected an answer. Lonny couldn't give her one. He never did; he never would. But unlike the other times she'd spoken to him, she needed a response, even though expecting one was totally illogical.

With every breath she drew, Robin knew that, but the futility of it all hit her, anyway. Her frustration came, so hard and unexpectedly powerful that it felt like a body blow. Robin closed her eyes, hoping the warmth of the sun would take away this bitter ache, this dreadful loneliness.

She felt so empty. Hollow all the way through.

Her fists clenched at her sides as tears filled her eyes. Embarrassed, she glanced around, grateful that the film crew had attracted most of the sightseers. No one was around to witness her distress. She brushed the tears from her cheeks.

Anger, which for so many years had lain dormant inside her, gushed forth in an avalanche of grief and pain. The tears spilled down her cheeks. Her lips quivered. Her shoulders shook. Her hands trembled.

It was as if the emotion was pounding against her chest and she was powerless to do anything but stand there and bear it.

The anger consumed her now. Consumed her because she hadn't allowed it to when Lonny was first killed. It had been more important to put on a brave front. More important to hold herself together for Jeff and for Lonny's parents. More important to deal with the present than confront the past.

Lonny had died and Robin was furious with him for leaving her alone with a child to raise. Leaving her alone to deal with filing taxes and taking out the garbage and repairing leaking pipes. All these years she'd managed on her own. And she'd bottled the anger up inside, afraid of ever letting it go.

"Robin."

Cole's voice, soft and urgent, reached out from behind her. At the sound, she turned and walked into his arms, sobbing, needing his comfort and his love in equal measure. Needing him as she'd never needed anyone before.

She didn't know how long he held her. He was whispering soothing words to her. Gentle words. But she heard none of them over the sound of her own suffering.

Once she started crying, Robin couldn't seem to stop. It was as if a dam had burst inside her and the anguish, stored for too many years, came pouring out.

Cole's arms were securely wrapped around her, shielding her. She longed to control this outburst, longed to explain, but every time she tried to speak her sobbing only grew worse.

"Let it out," he whispered. "You don't have to say anything. I understand."

"He doesn't answer," she sobbed. "I asked him... Lonny never answers me... because he can't. He left me..."

"He didn't want to die," Cole assured her.

"But he did... he did."

Cole didn't argue with her. He simply held her tenderly, stroking the back of her head as though reassuring a small child.

It took several minutes for Robin to compose herself enough to go on. "Part of me realizes that Lonny didn't want to leave me, didn't want to die. But he did and I'm so angry at him."

"That anger is what makes us human," Cole told her. He continued to comfort her and, gradually, bit by bit, Robin felt her composure slip back into place.

She sensed Jeff's presence even before he spoke.

"What wrong with my mom?" he asked Cole.

"She's dealing with some emotional pain," Cole explained, speaking as one adult to another.

"Is she going to be all right?"

Robin hadn't wanted her son to see her crying and made a concerted effort to break away from Cole, to reassure Jeff herself. Cole loosened his hold, but kept his arm around her shoulders.

"I'm fine, Jeff. Really."

"She doesn't look so good."

Her son had developed the irritating habit of not talking to her when she was upset. Jeff and Cole had done it that day her son had run away to the fort. He and Cole had carried on an entire conversation about her while she was in their midst then, too.

Cole led her to a bench and they all sat down.

Jeff plopped himself next to her and reached for her hand, patting it several times. Leaning toward Cole, he said earnestly, "Chocolate might help. One time Mom told me there wasn't anything in this world chocolate couldn't cure."

She'd actually said that? Robin started to smile. Wrapping her arms around her son, she hugged him close, loving him so much her heart seemed about to burst.

Jeff wasn't all that keen on being cuddled, especially in public, but although he squirmed, he put up with his mother's sudden need to hold him.

When she'd finished, Jeff rolled his eyes and once more directed his comments to Cole. "She gets weird like this every once in a while. Remember what happened that day I ran away?"

"I remember," Cole said, and Robin smiled at the trace of amusement she heard in his voice.

"Will you stop excluding me from this conversation? I'm going to be all right. I just had this overpowering need to cry, but don't worry, it's passed."

"See what I mean," Jeff muttered to Cole.

"But Jeff's right," Robin said, ignoring her son's comment. "Something chocolaty would definitely help."

"You'll be okay by yourself for a couple of minutes?" Cole asked.

"I'll be fine. I...don't know exactly what came over me, but I'm going to be just fine."

"I know you are." He kissed her, his lips gentle against her cheek.

The two of them left and once more Robin was alone. She didn't really understand why the pain and anger had hit her so hard now, after all this time. Except that it had something to do with Cole. But the last place she would ever have expected to give in to her grief was on Fisherman's Wharf with half of San Francisco looking on.

Jeff returned less than a minute later, running to her side with a double-decker chocolate ice-cream cone. "Cole's bringing two more for him and me," he explained. "I told the guy it was an emergency and he gave me this one right away."

"That was thoughtful of you," Robin said, wondering what the vendor must have thought. Smiling, she ran her tongue over the ice cream, savoring the cold chocolate. As profoundly as she'd wept, she felt almost giddy with relief now, repressing the urge to throw back her head and laugh.

Cole arrived, and with Jeff on her left and Cole on her right, she sat on the concrete bench and ate her ice-cream cone.

"I told you this would work," Jeff told Cole smugly.

"And to think I scoffed at your lucky baseball cap," she teased, feeling much better.

When they finished the cones, Cole gathered up their packages and led them back to where he'd parked his car.

Blackie was there to greet them the instant they returned to Orchard Street. Jeff ran into the backyard to play with the dog, and Cole walked Robin to her door. He accepted her offer of coffee.

"I'm probably going to be leaving soon for my property," he said, watching her closely. He sat down at the table, his hands cupping the mug as though to warm them. "Will you be all right?"

Robin nodded. She walked over and stood beside him and pressed a hand to his strong jaw. "I realize you delayed going up there today because of Jeff and his baseball game. We're both grateful.''

Cole placed his hand over hers and harshly expelled his breath. "I feel responsible for what you went through there on the pier. I should never have said what I did. I'm sorry, Robin, it wasn't any of my business.''

"You only said what I needed to hear.''

He smiled. "If I did, it was because of what happened to me in Seattle. I find it more than a little amazing that the two of us would come to grips with our pain while standing on a pier—me in Seattle, you here in San Francisco. I returned home with this incredible sense of release. For the first time since Bobby and Janice's deaths, I surrendered my grief. In a way it was as though I reached up and God reached down and together we came to an understanding.''

That so completely described what Robin had been feeling that for a long moment she couldn't say anything. What Cole had told her earlier about carrying the pain with her, dragging it everywhere she went, was right on the mark, too. He understood; he'd done the same thing himself. A surge of love swelled within her.

"I know you don't want to hear this,'' he was saying. "I honestly don't mean to pressure you. But once I returned from Seattle and realized I was falling in love with you I started thinking about having another baby.'' He hesitated and took a gulp of his coffee the way a thirsty man attacks a cold beer. He stood up abruptly, nearly knocking the chair backward. "I better go before I say or do something else I shouldn't.''

Robin followed him into the entryway, not wanting him to leave, but not quite ready to give him what he needed.

He paused at the screen door and his eyes immediately found hers. He couldn't seem to keep himself from touching her, brushing an auburn curl from her cheek. His knuckles grazed her skin lightly, and Robin's eyes closed of their own accord at the sensation that shot through her. Her heart was full, and she seemed to have all the answers now—except to the one question that was the most important in her life. And Jeff's.

"I'll see you next week some time," Cole said roughly, pulling his hand away. Without another word, he walked out the door, pausing at the top of the porch steps.

He called for his dog and in response both Blackie and Jeff came running.

"You're not leaving, are you?" Jeff asked breathlessly.

"I'm taking Blackie for the rest of the weekend. You think you can get along without him till Monday, sport?"

Jeff shrugged and stuck his fingers in the hip pockets of his blue jeans. "I suppose. Where are you taking him?"

"To my property." Cole didn't turn toward Robin. It was as if he had to ignore her in order to walk away from her.

"Oh, yeah!" Jeff said enthusiastically. "I remember your saying something about it once. You're building a house, aren't you?"

"Remodeling one. My grandfather lived there as a boy and he willed it to me, only it's been a lot of years since anyone's properly cared for that old house and there's plenty of work that needs to be done.''

"I'll work for you,'' Jeff piped in eagerly. He made up a fist and flexed his arm, revealing the meager muscles. "I know it doesn't look like much, but I'm strong. Just ask anyone.''

Cole tested Jeff's muscles, pretending to be impressed. "Yes, I can tell you're strong, and I'm sure I couldn't ask for a harder worker.'' Jeff beamed until Cole added regretfully, "I'll take you up there another time, sport.''

Jeff's face fell with disappointment.

Before she even realized what she was doing, Robin moved onto the porch. "Cole.''

He turned to face her, but the movement seemed reluctant.

Perhaps it was because she didn't want to be separated from him any more than he wanted to be away from her. Perhaps it was the thought of Jeff's being disappointed when he'd already had so many other disappointments in his young life. Perhaps it was this newborn sense of freedom she was just beginning to experience.

She stepped toward Cole. "Could Jeff and I go up to the property with you?''

Jeff didn't wait for Cole to answer before leaping excitedly into the air. "Hey, Mom, that's a great idea! Really great. Can we, Cole? Blackie and I can help you, and Mom can... Well, she can do things like make us some grub and bring us lemonade and other stuff women do when their men are working.''

"I'll have you both know I pound a mean hammer,'' Robin felt obliged to inform them. If she was going to Cole's farm, she fully intended to do her share.

Cole looked perplexed for a moment, as if he wasn't sure he'd heard her correctly. "I'd love to have you come—if you're sure that's what you want."

Robin just nodded. All she knew was that she couldn't bear to be separated from him any longer.

"Just be warned the house is only half done. The plumbing isn't in yet."

"We'll manage, won't we, Jeff?"

"Sure," Jeff said eagerly. "Anyway, boys got it easy."

Cole laughed. "How long will it take you to pack?"

"We're ready now, aren't we, Blackie?" Jeff almost jitterbugged across the front lawn in his enthusiasm.

"Give me a few minutes to throw some things together," Robin said, grinning. Jeff was smiling, too, ear to ear, as he raced past her into the house and up the stairs.

Cole's eyes held Robin's in silent communication—until Jeff came bursting out of the house, dragging his sheets and comforter with him, straight from his bed.

"Jeff," she cried, aghast, "what are you doing?"

"I took everything off my bed. I'm willing to go without plumbing, but I need certain comforts." He piled the bedding at their feet. "You two can go back to looking at each other. I'll get everything else we need."

"Jeff," Robin groaned, casting Cole an apologetic glance. "I'll pack my own things, thank you."

"You want me to get your sheets, too?" he called from inside the house.

"No." She scooped up the bedding and dashed into the house, taking the stairs two at a time. She discovered Jeff sitting on the edge of her bed, his expression pensive.

"What's wrong?"

"Are you ever going to marry Cole?" her son asked.

At the unexpectedness of the question, Robin's heart flew to her throat, then slid back into place. Briefly she wondered if Cole had brought up the subject with her son, but instinctively knew that he hadn't. "W-what makes you ask that?"

He shrugged. "Lots of things. Every time I turn around you two are gazing into each other's eyes. Either that, or kissing. I try to pretend I don't notice, but it's getting as bad as some of those movies you like to rent. And when you were crying on the pier, I saw something. Cole had his arms around you and he was looking real sad. Like...like he wished he could do the crying for you. It's the same look Grandpa sometimes gives Grandma when he figures out how she feels about something, and she doesn't even have to talk. Do you know what I mean?"

"I think so," Robin said, casually walking over to her dresser drawer and taking out a couple of old sweatshirts. "And what would you think if I said I was considering marrying Cole?"

Robin expected shouts of glee and wild shrieks, but instead, her son crossed his arms over his chest and moved his mouth in odd ways, stretching it sharply to one side and then the other. "You're serious, aren't you?"

"Yes." She folded and refolded one of the sweat-shirts, her heart pounding in anticipation. "It would mean a lot of changes for all of us."

"How many other people are involved in this?"

Robin hesitated, not understanding Jeff's concern. "What do you mean?"

"Will I get an extra set of grandparents in this deal?"

"Uh...probably. I haven't talked to Cole about that yet, but I assume so."

"That means extra gifts on my birthday and at Christmas. If that's the case, I say we should go for it."

"Jeffrey Leonard Masterson, you shock me!"

"A kid thinks that way. It shouldn't come as any surprise."

Robin shook her head in dismay at her son's sudden materialistic attitude toward her possible marriage. She was still frowning as she stepped outside.

Cole was in his garage, loading up the trunk of his four-wheel-drive vehicle when Robin joined him. She handed him one small suitcase and a bag of groceries she'd packed at the last moment.

Cole stowed them away, carefully avoiding her eyes. "I take it you said something to Jeff about us?" She could hear amusement in his voice.

"Yes. How'd you know?"

"He brought down a paper bag full of clothes, and asked what kind of presents he could expect from my parents at Christmas. He also asked if there were any aunts or uncles in the deal." Robin's embarrassment must have showed, because Cole started chuckling.

"That boy's got a mercenary streak in him I knew nothing about," she muttered.

Cole was still grinning. "You ready?"

She nodded, drawing an unsteady breath, eager for this adventure to begin. Jeff and Blackie were already in the back seat when Robin slipped in the front to wait for Cole.

"Are we going to sing camp songs?" Jeff asked, bracing his elbows on the back of their seats and leaning forward. He didn't wait for a response, but immediately launched into the timeless ditty about bottles of beer on the wall. He sang ninety-nine verses of that, then performed a series of other songs until they exited the freeway and wound up on a narrow country road with little traffic.

Jeff had tired of singing by then. "Knock knock," he called out.

"Who's there," Robin said, falling in with his game.

"Eisenhower."

"Eisenhower who?"

Jeff snickered. "Eisenhower late, how about you?" With that, the ten-year-old broke into belly-gripping guffaws, as if he should be receiving awards for his ability to tell jokes.

Cole's mouth was twitching and Robin had to admit that she was amused, too.

"The turnoff for the ranch is about a mile up the road," Cole explained. "Now remember, this is going to be a lot like camping. It's still pretty primitive."

"You don't need to worry," Robin said, smiling at him.

A couple of minutes later, Cole slowed about to turn down the long driveway. It was then that Robin saw the sign. Her heart jumped to her throat and her hands started to shake.

"Stop!" she screamed. "Stop!"

Cole slammed on the brakes, catapulting them forward. "Robin, what is it?"

Robin threw open the front door and leapt out of the car, running to the middle of the road. She stared at the one word on the sign even as the tears filled her eyes.

Cole's farm was named *Paradise*.

CHAPTER ELEVEN

"ROBIN, I DON'T UNDERSTAND," Cole said for the third time. His dark eyes were filled with worry.

"I bet my allowance she's crying again," Jeff muttered, poking his head out the side window. "Something weird's going on with my mother. She's been acting goofy all day. What do you think it is?"

"I'm not really sure," Cole said as he continued to study Robin.

For her part, Robin couldn't take her eyes off the sign. Jeff was right about her crying; the tears streamed unrestrained down her face. But these were tears of joy. Tears of gratitude. Tears of acknowledgment. It was exactly as Cole had described. She'd reached up and God had reached down and together they'd come to an understanding. She'd finally resolved her dilemma with Cole.

Unable to stop herself, Robin hurled her arms around Cole's neck. Her hands roamed his face. His wonderful, wonderful face.

Because her eyes were blurred with emotion, she couldn't accurately read Cole's expression, but it didn't matter. Her heart spilled over with love for him.

"Robin..."

She didn't let him finish, but began spreading a long series of kisses across his face, starting with his eyelids. "I love you, I love you," she repeated between kisses, moving from his cheek to his nose and downward.

Cole put his arms around her waist and pulled her closer. Robin was half-aware of the car door slamming and Jeff marching onto the road to join them.

"Are you two going to get all mushy on me again?"

Robin barely heard her son. Her mouth had unerringly found Cole's. When the kiss ended, his teeth tugged gently at her lower lip.

The unexpected sharp sound of a hand clap brought her out of her dream world. Her eyes immediately went to Jeff, who was looking very much like a pint-size adult. His face and eyes were as stern as she'd ever seen them.

"Do the two of you realize where you're standing?" Jeff demanded as though he'd recently been hired by the state police to make sure this type of thing didn't happen. "There are proper places to kiss, but the middle of the road isn't one of them."

"He's right," Cole said, his eyes devouring Robin. He didn't want to release her and did so with a reluctance that tugged at her heart.

"Come with me," Jeff said, taking his mother firmly by the hand and leading her back to the car. He paused in front of the door and glanced at Cole. "She might have a fever. She acts a little weird sometimes, but it's never been as bad as today."

"Robin," Cole said, grasping her hand, "can you explain now?"

She nodded. "It's the sign—Paradise. Tell me about it. Tell me why your grandfather named his place Paradise."

"I'm not entirely sure," Cole said, puzzled. "He lived here his whole life and always said this land was all he'd ever needed. From what I remember, he once told me he thought of this place as the Garden of Eden. I can only assume that's why he named it Paradise.''

Robin nodded, unsurprised by his explanation. "When Lonny and I were first married, we talked...we dreamed about someday buying some land and raising animals. Enough land for Jeff to have a pony and for me to have a huge garden. We decided this land would be our own piece of heaven on earth and...from that we came up with the idea of naming it Paradise.''

Slowly Cole shook his head, and she could tell he didn't completely understand.

"This afternoon, when I was standing on Fisherman's Wharf, you suggested I talk over my feelings about our getting married with Lonny.''

"What I suggested," Cole reminded her gently, "was that you *imagine* what he'd say to advise you. I certainly didn't expect you to really communicate with him.''

"I know this won't make any sense to you, but I've talked to Lonny lots of times over the years. This afternoon, what hit me so hard was the fact that Lonny would never answer me. That realization was what finally forced me to deal with the pain. To forgive Lonny for dying.''

Jeff was looking at her as if he was about to suggest they call a doctor.

"Here you were wanting to marry me and I didn't know what to do. I had trouble believing your proposal was prompted by anything more than the desire to replace the family you'd lost. I do love you, and I desperately wanted to believe you loved me—and Jeff. But I wasn't sure...."

"And you're sure now?"

She nodded enthusiastically. "Yes. With all my heart, I'm confident that marrying you would be the right thing for all of us."

"Of course we're going to marry Cole!" Jeff cried. "Good grief, if you had any doubts, all you had to do was ask me and I would've told you. It's obvious we belong together."

"Yes, it is, isn't it," Robin whispered. "Cole," she said, gripping both his hands with her own. "I'd consider it a very great honor to become your wife."

"Jeff?" Cole said, tearing his eyes away from Robin. "I want to know what you think."

The boy's face beamed and his eyes sparkled. "I'd consider it a very great honor to become your son."

Cole brushed his lips across Robin's and then reached for Jeff, hauling him into his arms and squeezing him tight. Blackie started barking then, wanting out of the car. Robin quickly moved to open the passenger door, and the black Lab leapt out. She crouched down and wrapped her arms around his thick neck, hugging him. "You're going to have a whole family now, Blackie," she murmured happily.

TWO HOURS LATER, just at dusk, Robin was standing in the middle of the yard. She'd loved everything about Paradise, just as she'd known she would. The house and property were nothing like the place she and Lonny had dreamed about, but she hadn't expected them to be. The four-bedroom house was much larger than anything they'd ever hoped to own. The land was filled with Ponderosa pine trees, and the rocky ground was more suitable to grazing a few sheep or cattle than planting crops.

Cole was showing Jeff the barn, and Robin had intended to join them, but the evening was filled with a sweet-smelling breeze and she'd stopped to breathe in the fresh cool air. She folded her arms and stood there, smiling into the clear sky. A multitude of twinkling stars were just beginning to reveal themselves.

Cole walked quietly up behind her, and slipped his arms around her waist, pulling her against him. "Have I told you how much I love you?"

"In the last fifteen minutes? No, you haven't."

"Then allow me to correct that situation." He nibbled the back of her neck gently. "I love you to distraction."

"I love you, too."

He sighed then, and whispered hoarsely, "It was a difficult decision to marry me, wasn't it?"

Robin agreed with a nod.

"Had I given you so many reasons to doubt me?"

"No," she said quickly, turning in his arms. She pressed her palms against his jaw. "I had to be sure in my heart you weren't trying to replace the son you'd lost with Jeff. And I had to be equally certain you loved me for myself and not because I was Jeff's mother and we came as a package deal."

He shook his head decisively. "Jeff's a great kid, don't get me wrong, but there's never been any doubt in my mind how I felt about you. The first time we met, you hit me square between the eyes. I didn't mean to fall in love again. I didn't even want it."

"I don't think I did, either," Robin confessed.

"Past experience had taught us both that loving someone only causes pain. I loved Janice, but I could never make her happy. When we divorced I accepted my part in the breakup."

"But she had a drinking problem, Cole. You can't blame yourself."

"I don't, not entirely, but I accept a portion of the blame for what went wrong. It tore me apart to see Bobby caught in the middle, and in an effort to minimize the pain I didn't fight for custody. He was an innocent victim of the divorce, and I didn't want him to suffer any further distress. I was willing to do anything I could to spare him. Later, when I realized how serious Janice's problem with alcohol had become, I tried to obtain custody, but before I could get the courts to move on it, the accident happened. Afterward, I was left to deal with the guilt of having waited too long.

"The thought of ever marrying again, having children again, terrified me. I couldn't see making myself vulnerable a second time." He paused, and a slow, gentle smile spread across his face, smoothing away the tension. "All that changed when I met you. It was as if life was offering me a second chance. And I knew I had to grab hold of it with both hands or forever live with regret."

"Oh, brother," Jeff said as he dashed into the yard. "Are you two at it again?"

"We're talking," Robin explained.

"Your mouths are too close together for talking." He strolled past them, Blackie at his side. "I don't suppose you thought about making me anything to eat, did you, Mom?"

"I made sandwiches."

"Great. Are there enough for Blackie to have one?"

"I think so. There's cans of pop and some corn chips in the kitchen, too."

"Great," Jeff repeated, hurrying into the house.

"Are you hungry?" Robin asked Cole.

"Yes," he stated emphatically, "but my appetite doesn't seem to be for food. How long will you keep me waiting to make you my wife?"

"I'll have to call my parents and my brother and make the arrangements. It's important to me that we have a church wedding. It doesn't have to be fancy, but I'd like to invite a handful of good friends and—"

"How long?"

"To make the arrangements? I'm not exactly sure. Three, possibly four months to do it properly. Maybe longer."

"One month," Cole said.

"What do you mean, one month?"

"I'm giving you exactly thirty days to arrange whatever you want, but that's as long as I'm willing to wait."

"But, Cole—"

He swept her into his arms then and his mouth claimed hers in a fury of desire. Robin found herself trembling and she clutched his shirt, her fingers bunching the material as she strove to regain her equilibrium.

"Cole..." She felt chilled and feverish at the same time. Needy, yet wealthy beyond her wildest dreams.

"One month?" he repeated.

"One month," she agreed, pressing her face against his broad warm chest. They'd both loved, profoundly, and they'd lost what they'd valued most. For years, in their own ways, they'd sealed themselves off from others, because no one else could understand their pain. Then they'd found one another, and nothing would ever be the same again. Their love was the mature love that comes when one has suffered and lost and been left to rebuild a shattered life. The love they shared was stronger than either could ever have hoped for.

"Do you see what I was telling you about?" Jeff muttered to Blackie, sitting on the back porch steps. "I suppose we're going to have to put up with this for a while."

Blackie munched on a corn chip, apparently more interested in sharing Jeff's meal than listening to his comments.

"I can deal with it, if you can," Jeff continued. "I suspect I'll be getting at least one brother out of this deal, and if we're lucky maybe two. A sister would be all right, too, I guess—" he sighed deeply "—but I'll have to think about that. Girls can be a real headache, if you know what I mean."

The dog wagged his tail as Jeff slipped him another corn chip. "And you know what, Blackie? It's gonna be Father's Day soon. My very first. And I've already got a card picked out. It's got a picture of a father, a mother and a little boy with a baseball cap. And there's a dog on it that looks just like you!"

FIRST CLASS

Coming soon
to an easy chair near you.

FIRST CLASS is Harlequin's armchair travel plan for the incurably romantic. You'll visit a different dreamy destination every month from January through December without ever packing a bag. No jet lag, no expensive air fares and *no* lost luggage. Just First Class Harlequin Romance reading, featuring exotic settings from Tasmania to Thailand, from Egypt to Australia, and more.

FIRST CLASS romantic excursions guaranteed! Start your world tour in January. Look for the special **FIRST CLASS** destination on selected Harlequin Romance titles—there's a new one every month.

NEXT DESTINATION:
FLORENCE, ITALY

Harlequin Books

JTR7

Back by Popular Demand

Janet Dailey
Americana

A romantic tour of America through fifty favorite Harlequin
Presents® novels, each set in a different state researched by
Janet and her husband, Bill. A journey of a lifetime in one
cherished collection.

In June, don't miss the sultry states featured in:

Title # 9 - FLORIDA
        Southern Nights
    #10 - GEORGIA
        Night of the Cotillion

Available wherever
Harlequin books are sold.

JD-JR

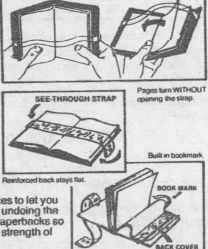

Harlequin Books®

GREAT NEWS...
HARLEQUIN UNVEILS NEW SHIPPING PLANS

For the convenience of customers, Harlequin has announced that Harlequin romances will now be available in stores at these convenient times each month*:

Harlequin Presents, American Romance, Historical, Intrigue:

> May titles: April 10
> June titles: May 8
> July titles: June 5
> August titles: July 10

Harlequin Romance, Superromance, Temptation, Regency Romance:

> May titles: April 24
> June titles: May 22
> July titles: June 19
> August titles: July 24

We hope this new schedule is convenient for you.

With only two trips each month to your local bookseller, you'll never miss any of your favorite authors!

*Please note: There may be slight variations in on-sale dates in your area due to differences in shipping and handling.

HDATES-R